Starscape Books by David Lubar

NOVELS

Flip

My Rotten Life: Nathan Abercrombie, Accidental Zombie, Book One

Dead Guy Spy: Nathan Abercrombie, Accidental Zombie, Book Two

Hidden Talents

True Talents

STORY COLLECTIONS

The Battle of the Red Hot Pepper Weenies
and Other Warped and Creepy Tales

The Curse of the Campfire Weenies
and Other Warped and Creepy Tales

In the Land of the Lawn Weenies
and Other Warped and Creepy Tales

Invasion of the Road Weenies
and Other Warped and Creepy Tales

Nathan Abercrombie,
Accidental Zombie

BOOK THREE

GOOP
SOUP

David Lubar

A Tom Doherty Associates Book · New York

GOOP SOUP

Copyright © 2010 by David Lubar

The Big Stink excerpt copyright © 2010 by David Lubar

Reader's Guide copyright © 2010 by Tor Books

A Starscape Book
Published by Tom Doherty Associates, LLC
175 Fifth Avenue
New York, NY 10010

www.tor-forge.com

ISBN 978-0-7653-1636-3 (hardcover)
ISBN 978-0-7653-2509-9 (trade paperback)

First Edition: May 2010

Printed in March 2010 in the United States of America by RR Donnelley, Harrisonburg, Virginia

0 9 8 7 6 5 4 3 2 1

For my distant cousin, Steve Schlossman; his wonderful wife, Barbara Dennard; and my sometimes-less-distant cousin, Mikhael Schlossman

CONTENTS

INTRODUCTION

I used to think life was hard. Now I know better: Life is simple. Death is tricky.

1

Stool Pigeon

When the pigeon shot into our classroom, most of the boys shouted, "Whoa!" About half the girls shouted, "Eewwww!"

Our teacher, Ms. Delambre, shouted, "My goodness!"

That's the sort of thing adults say when they're trying not to use bad words. My friend Mookie and I grinned at each other. His mom says *my goodness* a lot.

I didn't shout anything until the pigeon swooped down from the ceiling and landed on my left shoulder.

"Hey! Get off!"

It didn't.

I reached up to push it away, but I was afraid I

might hurt it. I read somewhere that birds have hollow bones. I knew how that felt. My own bones break pretty easily.

They weren't always like that. I was a normal kid until I got splashed with Hurt-Be-Gone and turned into a half-dead zombie by my friend Abigail's crazy uncle Zardo. Now I don't have a heartbeat. But much to my surprise, that hasn't been too big a problem.

The pigeon turned its head and stared at me.

I stared back.

The pigeon blinked.

I didn't.

That's another thing I don't need to do. Though I try to remember to make myself blink once in a while so I don't creep people out.

The pigeon's tail twitched. Something wet and white plopped on my shirt, right across my pocket.

"Great. Thanks a lot," I told the pigeon.

I'd just been turned into a living statue. What next? Maybe the pigeon would build a nest in my hair and lay eggs.

As kids all around me collapsed in laughter, pointed at my shirt, and made bad jokes about pigeon poop, the bird fluttered off my shoulder and swooped back out the window.

Mookie, who was sitting next to me, laughed so hard, he fell off his stool. And he fell so hard, he bounced. I guess he didn't get hurt, because he kept laughing.

Only Abigail wasn't laughing. She turned toward the window, watched the pigeon, and tugged at the ends of her frizzy dark brown hair. She's so smart, it's almost scary. But she never shows off in school.

"All right, class!" Ms. Delambre said. "That's quite enough. Settle down. This is science class—not party time." She walked over to me and pointed at the blotch on my shirt. "Nathan, go wash that off immediately. Pigeon droppings carry all sorts of diseases."

I hopped down from my stool and headed for the sink in the back of the room. I could feel two dozen pairs of eyes following me. I wasn't worried about germs. I was pretty sure I couldn't get any kind of disease. And even if I did, it couldn't hurt me. But I still didn't want that stuff on my shirt. Mom is always telling me to be careful about getting food on my clothes. If she ever sat through a lunch period in the school cafeteria, she'd know how impossible that is.

I grabbed a paper towel and wiped at the stain. I expected the blob to smear. But it stuck to the paper towel and slid right off my pocket.

What in the world? . . .

I realized it was a piece of plastic. There was something printed on the back side in tiny letters. I looked closer.

URGENT MISSION COMING. MAJOR OPERATION. BE READY TO SPRING INTO ACTION. P.M.

P.M. That had to be Peter Murphy—the spy who'd recruited me to work for the Bureau of Useful Misadventures. BUM looks for kids who mess up in some kind of way that makes them good spies. They also fight to make the world a better place. That's their mission, though I'm still not sure exactly what it means.

I looked over toward Ms. Delambre. She was trying to close the window, but it was stuck. She usually kept it open, because the room always got too hot, even when it was cold outside.

I crumpled up the paper towel and tossed it in the trash. Urgent mission? Cool. That was exciting, and also a little scary. I was going to get my first real spy assignment from BUM. Nathan Abercrombie, Super Spy. This is the job I was born for. Or died for, I guess.

I hoped this new mission was important. I'd already done one job for BUM, but that was just a quick little thing. I'd climbed a fence and put a package in a building. At the time, I didn't have a clue what was going on. Even so, I'd ended up saving a lot of people. That felt so good, it made me want to do more spy stuff. Being a spy was sort of like being dropped in the middle of an action video game.

I returned to our lab table. Mookie had gotten back onto his stool, but he was still choking down snorts and spitting out chuckles. He sounded like a steam engine that was in danger of exploding—a short, round steam engine with large square glasses and shaggy light brown hair.

"It's not that funny," I said.

He shook his head. "It's more than funny. It's like mega-funny. No, giga-funny. Wait—what comes after giga?"

"Tera," Abigail said.

"Tera-funny?" Mookie frowned, then said it a couple more times, like he was trying to taste the words. "Nope. Sounds too serious. I'll stick with giga-funny, 'cause that sounds like giggles. And seeing Nate get splattered really makes me giggle." He started laughing again.

Abigail tapped my arm. "I assume the pigeon was delivering a message from BUM." She and Mookie were the only people who knew about my secret life as a soon-to-be spy. The other kids in school didn't even know I was a zombie. To them I was just plain old Nathan Abercrombie, the second-skinniest kid in class.

"Yeah. They have a mission for me. Something big. How'd you know it wasn't a real bird?"

"Wing speed and movement," Abigail said. "Real pigeons don't fly that way. They don't crash and burn, either. That one flew smack into the phone pole." She pointed out the window.

I leaned toward the window and spotted the smoldering remains of the mechanical bird on the street.

"Why can't they just call me on the phone or send an e-mail?" I asked. BUM loved using all sorts of robots and high-tech equipment. It didn't seem to bother them that most of it blew up or caught on fire.

Abigail sighed. "Boys and their toys. Even when they grow up, they have to play."

"Well, yeah," I said. "Toys are cool."

Mookie stopped laughing and poked my shoulder. He opened his mouth to say something, then lost control again.

"Just say it," I told him. I was getting tera-tired of this.

"Are you exhausted?" he asked.

"You know I don't need to sleep." That was actually the best part about being half-dead—I could stay up all night and play computer games. Or do other things—if I ever figured out something better to do.

"But you must be really really really exhausted," he said.

I didn't want to ask, but he was my best friend, and I could tell he was dying to do this. "Okay, why do you think I'm exhausted?"

"Because you look *pooped!*"

He fell off his stool again. Ms. Delambre, who'd given up trying to close the window and returned to her desk, made him sit in the hallway for the rest of science class. She let him in for math, but he didn't last long before he got sent back into the hall.

"Are you finished?" I asked as we headed outside for recess.

"I'm not sure. I mean, you have to admit it's pretty funny."

"Hilarious," I said. "But maybe it's time to drop it."

"Drop!" He pointed at my shirt, then started laughing again. "The pigeon already dropped it!"

He was like that for the rest of the day. All through recess, he kept grabbing the ends of his jacket and stretching his arms out, making wings. "I'm MookieHawk!" he shouted. "Don't mess with me, or I'll mess your shirt." He'd flap his arms a couple times, race over to me, scream, "PLOP!" and then fall down laughing.

"He looks more like MookieCanary," Abigail said.

She was right. Mookie was wearing a bright yellow jacket that was about two or three sizes too large for him. His mom had won it last month on a radio call-in contest. There was a big ad on the back for Colonel Esterol's Deep-Fried Pizza Parlor. It showed a smiling slice of pizza— complete with skinny arms and legs—happily swimming the backstroke in a vat of boiling oil. Kids made fun of it, but Mookie didn't seem to care.

By the end of recess, he must have fallen about twenty times. But that was okay. Even though he kept kidding me, I was happy the rest of the day, thinking about my first spy mission.

At least, I was happy until that evening, when Mom hit me with the worst possible news a half-dead zombie kid could hear.

2

No Sweat

Mom works at a store in the mall where people make their own teddy bears. Stuffy Wuffy. When anyone asks me what my mom does, I just shrug and say, "Stuff." Which is true. She helps people stuff their bears. She also helps them pick out bear heads, bear arms, bear legs, and cute little bear sweatshirts.

I asked her once if she could make me a bear that was just four heads stitched together without a body, but she didn't seem to understand how awesome that would be—especially if they looked like they were screaming.

Dad is an accountant. He likes to say that he crunches numbers. I can picture him sitting at a desk with a big cereal bowl full of numbers and milk, spooning them into his mouth and crunching down. Every number would have a different fruit flavor. Dad works late a lot. But today, he got home before Mom.

"How about a quick run?" he asked after he'd put his briefcase down on the kitchen table.

"Sure." We'd gotten into the habit of running whenever Dad had time. Since I didn't need to breathe, and since my muscles never felt tired, running was my best sport.

"Great. I'll get into my sweats."

While Dad was changing, I grabbed the plastic bag I'd hidden in the upstairs bathroom. I kept a piece of sponge in there that I'd gotten from under the kitchen sink. The sponge was pretty dry, so I added some water, then stuck the bag in my pocket. I went back to the kitchen and waited for Dad.

"How was school?" he asked as we jogged down the street.

"Good. I got an A on my spelling test." I got good grades on most of my tests. Since I didn't need to sleep, I had way too much free time, so I killed a chunk of it each night by studying.

"Excellent. If you want, we could celebrate by going bowling this weekend. We haven't done that in a while."

I liked bowling, but I realized it would be a very bad idea. I'd already lost fingers a couple times, and had to glue them back on. I could just imagine the bowling ball flying down the alley, taking my thumb and two fingers with it. I'd have just enough fingers left to give that surfer-dude *Rock on!* sign.

"I'm sort of tired of bowling," I said. "Is that okay?"

"Absolutely. We could do something else. Whatever you feel like is fine with me."

"Anything?"

"Just about. Though I don't think your mom will let me take you parasailing. Speaking of excitement, ready to get the heart pumping?"

"Sure."

He picked up the speed. I followed along.

When we reached the end of the next block, I slipped my hand into my pocket, opened the bag, and sneaked the sponge into my palm. I pretended to scratch my neck, pressing down on the sponge enough to get some water on my shirt.

Just like that, I had instant fake sweat. If I finished our run with a dry shirt, Dad might figure out that something was wrong. Even if Dad didn't notice my lack of sweat, Mom would definitely spot it if she got home before we did. She pays far too much attention to me.

It wasn't easy being dead around Mom. I had to spend a lot of my time pretending to be alive. Whenever she was home, I made sure to go into the bathroom once in a while, even though I didn't need to. I pushed my food around and made it look like I was eating. I did all kinds of things just to keep my parents from learning I was dead.

"Want to cut across on the new road?" Dad asked when we reached the top of the hill. They were building some houses near us, and had just started bulldozing the road. A lot of people had moved out of town, but the new people who moved here seemed to want bigger houses. So somebody was building them.

I nodded, and followed Dad through the development. All around us, I saw the skeletons of houses. Some had walls, but others were just empty frames. A moment later, I heard a strange sound.

Smack. Scrape. Smack. Scrape.

Dad and I stopped and looked around. The sound stopped. I started running again.

Smack. Scrape. Smack. Scrape.

I kept running, but glanced down.

Oh no.

I'd stepped on a nail with my left foot. That wouldn't have been too bad, since I don't feel pain. Except that the nail was stuck through a small square board. And now the board was nailed to my foot. I could see the point of the nail sticking up through the top of my sneaker. It had gone all the way through my foot. I kept jogging and tried to shake the board off. That didn't work. The board just spun on the nail like a propeller on a cheap toy airplane.

Dad was still looking around. Mom likes to say that Dad couldn't find water in a rainstorm. She's sort of right. He doesn't pay much attention to things around him. And he's the last person you want to ask to find the jar of pickles in the fridge. But the way the board was spinning and flapping, he'd notice it any second. I had to do something right away. I put my left foot flat on the sidewalk, stomped down on the board with my right foot, and yanked my left leg up hard. The nail pulled loose.

I started to jog away.

Dad glanced back, then turned and jogged over to the board. He picked it up and stared at it. "Are you all right?"

"Yeah." I laughed to show him I wasn't in pain. Of course, I'm never in pain anymore, except when I use my special glue to stick broken fingers back on. "Boy, that was close. It missed my foot. Pretty lucky, huh?"

"Yeah. Pretty lucky." Dad tossed the board into a Dumpster near us. "So, what do you want to do this weekend?"

"Maybe we could play pool." That would be safe, as long as I didn't fall on a cue and impale myself.

I ran next to Dad and gave myself another squirt from the sponge. The rest of the way through the new road, I kept a careful watch for nails.

Dad let out a happy sigh at the end of our run and patted me on the back. "Life is good," he said.

"Yeah. Life is good."

I went upstairs and checked out my foot. There was a small hole through it, a couple inches behind my middle toe, but it didn't look too bad. After seeing the ends of my own broken fingers several times, a tiny hole wasn't a big deal at all.

I took a shower, even though I hadn't actually sweated. When you're dead, it's not a bad idea to try to stay clean. I put some soap on both ends of the hole, just in case, and rinsed it really well.

As I was turning off the water, something dark plopped onto my arm from the showerhead. "Great," I muttered. "The whole universe decided it's Plop Stuff on Nathan Day." I could just imagine large flocks of seagulls making their way toward East Craven. And bats. Lots of bats.

I stared at the glop on my arm. It was the size and shape of a gumdrop, and the color of the dark green sludge you find when you clean an aquarium filter. It quivered for a moment, like it was trying to keep its shape, and then it got softer and flowed across my arm.

Another large drop was hanging from the shower-head. I touched it with my finger. It was oily and thick, sort of like Mom's version of cooked spinach. Though there's no way it could be as deadly. Mom can cook all the health out of even the most nutritious vegetable.

I went to the sink and washed the goop off my arm and

finger. The water from the faucet seemed fine. I figured the dark stuff was just some kind of gunk that had built up in the showerhead. No big deal. I went back to my room and did my homework. By then, it was time for dinner.

Mom brought takeout from Random Wok. They have Chinese food, and all sorts of other Asian stuff, too, like sushi, pho, and pad Thai.

I was pushing some kung pao chicken around on my plate, pretending to eat, when Dad told Mom, "Nate and I went for a jog."

"That's wonderful," Mom said. "It was a beautiful day."

"We cut across the new road," he said. "Those builders really should be more careful."

Don't say it. I clutched my chopsticks and hoped Dad wouldn't give her the details.

"Careful?" Mom asked. "Why?"

Please don't tell her.

"He stepped on a rusty nail," Dad said.

NO! His words hung in the air for a moment. I wanted to grab them and stuff them under the couch cushions before Mom reacted. But I knew it was too late. There are some things that moms should never hear. *Rusty nail* is way up there near the top of the list, right next to *BB gun*, *pet snake*, and *cliff diving*.

"A rusty nail?" Mom screamed. "A rusty nail!" She leaped from her seat, dashed over to me, and grabbed my ankles. "Let me see?"

I felt like a horse that was about to get shoes. "It's nothing." I was really glad I'd taken off my sneakers and put on different socks, so there was no sign of the hole.

She grabbed the tops of my socks. "Let me see."

I pulled my feet away. "I'll do it."

I couldn't show her my left foot. I couldn't show her an uninjured foot, either. She'd know it was the wrong foot and ask to see the other one. I slipped off my right sock. As I did that, I scratched the bottom of my foot with my thumbnail.

"Look, it's nothing." I showed her the place I'd scratched.

"You can't take chances with rusty nails. You'll probably need a tetanus booster. I'm calling Dr. Scrivella's office right now. Maybe he can see you tonight." She grabbed her cell phone and headed for the hallway.

I'd had my yearly checkup with Dr. Scrivella a week or two before I'd become a zombie. I thought I was safe until next year. I'd be in big trouble if I had to see him now. If anyone could tell the living from the dead, it would be a doctor.

Mom came back from the hallway.

"Dr. Scrivella doesn't think it's an emergency," she said.

"Good. I told you I was okay." That was a relief.

"But I explained how concerned I was, and he wants to check you over, and maybe give you a shot. Don't make any plans for after school on Wednesday. You have an appointment."

I couldn't let the doctor get near me. He was really old, and his eyesight was awful, but he'd have to be dead himself not to figure out that I was a zombie.

Don't worry—he's just going to look at your foot and give you a shot. He won't notice that you're dead.

But I couldn't take that chance. Mom gets all overprotective if I sneeze or cough. She was totally freaking out about a tiny scratch from a rusty nail. I didn't know what she'd do if she found out I'd stopped breathing, sleeping, or feeling pain.

"I don't need an appointment," I said. "I'm fine."

"Oh, don't be such a baby," Dad said. "It won't hurt."

That was true. Dr. Scrivella could give me shots all day long with a basketball pump, and I wouldn't even flinch. "It's not that," I said. "I have this thing I have to do after school Wednesday."

"Do it some other time," Mom said.

"But . . ." I realized that stalling wouldn't help. If Mom wanted me to go to the doctor, I'd go to the doctor. One way or another, she'd make sure I got there.

So, that was my day. An unknown mission coming from BUM at an unknown time, and an appointment with Dr. Scrivella in less than two days.

BUM got in touch with me sooner than I expected. This time, they didn't use a fake pigeon. They used a laser beam.

3

Writing on the Wall

As I mentioned, I don't sleep. I still do all the regular stuff any kid does before bedtime, like brush my teeth and put on my pajamas. But I never fall asleep. I don't feel tired. Just bored sometimes.

I still haven't figured out the perfect way to kill all that extra time. Mostly, after my parents fall asleep, I get on the computer and play games. I'd been into role-playing games for a while, but I just found a site with all these awesome old-school platform games. So I was doing a lot of running, jumping, climbing, and diving.

Monday night, I didn't have a chance to get bored.

As I was sitting in bed, listening to my parents head off to their room, I noticed a flash out of the corner of my eye. Red letters appeared on my wall.

NATHAN
IF YOU SEE THIS
SWITCH YOUR LIGHT ON AND OFF

The letters had the flickery look of a laser. I switched my lamp off and on. The letters on my wall changed.

GO TO BUM

I put my clothes back on. I had a good escape route from my house—out the window, and then across the garage roof to the drainpipe. My parents slept on the other side of the house, so there wasn't much chance they'd hear me leave, unless I made a whole lot of noise. I'm not as clumsy as Mookie, but even when I try to be quiet, I sometimes bang around a bit.

The entrance to BUM is inside the Museum of Tile and Grout, which is on the other side of town from here. Luckily, East Craven is a small town. Our neighborhood is totally safe. Dad doesn't even lock the car when he leaves it in the driveway.

I thought about jogging to the museum, but I didn't want to attract too much attention. There were people out for walks. Some of them were just strolling. Others looked like they had places to go. None of them acted like they even noticed me.

The museum door was unlocked. The lady at the desk smiled at me, but she didn't stop knitting. I headed for the elevator. The door opened when I got close. I went inside and took a seat. The elevator is actually a high-speed car that shoots from East Craven to BUM headquarters, wherever that is.

Mr. Murphy was waiting for me at the end of my ride. He's tall, with big ears, red hair, and a bit too much enthusiasm for making fun of me.

"I still don't understand why you won't use e-mail," I said.

"I don't understand why there are so many different brands of blue jeans for sale," he said.

"Very funny." I reached into my pocket, pulled out my cell phone, and waved it in his face. My folks had gotten it for me last Christmas, after a year of nonstop begging. "Seriously, you could just call me. Or text me. And you don't wear jeans."

"Phone lines are not secure. E-mail isn't secure. Texting is absurdly slow and tedious. I can't risk letting our enemies learn about you. And, for your information, I happen to look quite splendid in jeans. But enough of that. You need to start preparing for your mission."

Mission. I liked the sound of that. "What will I be doing?"

"Infiltrating an enemy staging base. We want you to slip in, copy their computer files, and then slip out."

"What's a staging base?"

"That's where the bad guys set things up to carry out a mission," he said. "Sort of like their local headquarters."

"What enemy?"

"RABID."

"*RABBIT?* They don't sound very dangerous. Are they related to *BUNNY?*" I pictured a field of long-eared, twitchy-nosed spies wearing dark glasses and jabbing each other with pointed carrots.

"Not *RABBIT*. *RABID*. Raise Anarchy by Inciting Disorder. Th   ¹ to destroying freedom and democracy."

"Why?"

"That's a long, boring, and complicated story, Nathan. To tell the truth, politics often doesn't make much sense. And even when it makes sense, it can be quite depressing. I'll give you the short version. They want absolute power and total control. That can't happen as long as people are free."

I thought about that for a moment. Even though Mr. Murphy felt it was too complicated for me, it sounded sort of familiar. *Power and control.* Any fifth-grader knew all about that. "So, really, what they are is bullies," I said. *Or gym teachers.*

Mr. Murphy looked surprised. "Nathan, that's an

excellent way to put it. Bullies. Yes. It's not just people who can be bullies. Organizations can act like that, too. RABID is a bunch of bullies."

"And they're the bad guys you've been trying to stop?"

"They're one group of bad guys," Mr. Murphy said. "Unfortunately, there are many others. SPLOTCH has been giving us trouble in Europe. GACK has been quiet for a while, though we expect them to start up again soon in North Africa. MUCOUS, in Asia, is really causing problems. As is the Belgian branch of PHLEGM."

"That's a lot of bad guys," I said.

"It's a big world. But right now, RABID is especially dangerous, and especially difficult to defeat, because they work in small groups, spread all over the world. They have a central headquarters, but we've never managed to find it. Let me give you a better idea of what we're up against."

He led me to the room with the large flat screen. I'd been there before, watching a video about the important work BUM does. This time, instead of a video, Mr. Murphy put up a picture of a town.

"This is Gwinthmyr, a small town in Wales. Until fifteen years ago, it was a happy place. Then, suddenly, the air started to smell like garlic."

"I love garlic," I said.

"Many people do," Mr. Murphy said. "But nobody was happy about an endless aroma of garlic. People complained. The government looked into it and failed to find a cause. People started to dislike their local leaders more than usual. Fortunately, agents of one of our sister organizations discovered the device RABID had installed and destroyed it."

Mr. Murphy flipped through a series of other pictures.

"Adlesville, Ireland—a storage tank holding a hundred thousand gallons of molasses mysteriously ruptured, flooding the town knee-deep in syrup. Borman, Arizona—all cable and satellite TV stopped working. Perchangy, Australia—every sidewalk in town developed cracks and holes. Whamply, Canada—fifty thousand small toads invaded the town, clogging everything."

"The road must have gotten real slippery," I said.

"It wasn't pretty," Mr. Murphy said. "All of this was the work of RABID. This is only a small example of what they've done. Not to mention at least a dozen plots we've managed to stop over the past several years before they could be put into action."

"These guys really stink. I definitely want to help."

"Excellent. Come on—let's get to the lab. Dr. Cushing wants to explain something to you." He headed down the hallway.

I thought about all the dangerous stuff I'd seen at BUM headquarters. They'd collected it to keep it away from kids. BUM looked for kids who'd become useful as spies because of some sort of accident—like the one I'd had. The bad guys didn't just look for kids like me who'd had useful accidents—they made stuff that could cause accidents. "Does RABID make things that hurt kids?"

"That's one of the things they do. But it's not their main mission. They're much more interested in creating disorder for large groups of people than they are in creating misadventures."

"Where is this staging base?" I wondered whether I'd get to go to Europe or Asia. That would be awesome.

"We don't know the exact location yet."

"Doesn't that make it sort of hard to break in? I mean, if you don't know where the bad guys are, how can you go there?"

"We're working on it," he said. "Information tends to trickle in. The bad guys don't have a Web site. They don't run ads on TV. We have to patch things together from thousands of clues. Recent activity indicates RABID is planning something on the East Coast. We should know where they are very soon, even though we still have no idea what they're planning. I hope we'll be going into action by the end of this week. But we're getting ahead of ourselves. You need to train first."

"Train?"

"Of course. Unless you think you were born knowing how to be a spy. Were you? Did you appear on this planet knowing all there is to know about espionage?"

"Nope. But I've seen a lot of spy movies."

"I'm sure that will come in handy. But, as I was saying, a boy such as yourself, who has experienced a misadventure, can be very useful. And a trained spy can be very useful. But if you combine the two, you have an amazing agent." He patted my shoulder. "You are going to accomplish dazzling things, Nathan."

"Cool." I imagined myself learning to do all sorts of spy stuff, just like in the movies. Maybe they'd teach me to fly a helicopter. "When do I start training?"

"As soon as we're finished here."

We'd reached the lab. "Nathan, it's good to see you," Dr. Cushing said. "How have you been?" I noticed she'd gotten a couple highlights in her dark hair. Mom got highlights once in a while. I'm not sure what the point was of all that, but it did look pretty nice on Dr. Cushing.

"I've been okay. Any luck with the bone machine?" I asked. She was trying to develop a machine that would strengthen my bones.

"I'm working on it. And some other things that might make your life easier. But right now, I just wanted to explain a theory I had, so your first training session makes sense. Okay?"

"Sure." That's one of the reasons I liked her. Mr. Murphy tried to keep as much as possible a secret from everyone. Dr. Cushing explained things.

"Have you ever felt that someone was staring at you?" she asked.

"All the time now," I said. "I'm afraid they'll notice something is wrong and figure out I'm dead."

"Not like that," she said. "But when you're just sitting somewhere or walking, and you sense something."

"Yeah, sure." I knew what she meant. I'd feel eyes on

me, and a lot of the time, someone really was staring. It happened pretty often when Rodney was around. He was the biggest bully in the school—though he was still out sick, recovering from the high school wrestling disaster. Bullies had extra-strength stares. "What's that have to do with me?"

"There are aspects of life we don't understand," Dr. Cushing said. "People really do sense things we can't explain. Just like we can't explain how you can move your finger even when it isn't attached to your body. We're hoping that, since you aren't alive, you might be less easy to sense."

"Or maybe even senseless," Mr. Murphy said. He let out a giggle.

"How can you test that?" I asked.

"In the field," Mr. Murphy said. "We're going to take you out in the real world and see what happens."

4

Stare Case

I followed him back to the row of elevator doors. Instead of my usual door, a different one opened. There were two seats inside. "Where are we going?" I asked.

"It doesn't matter."

"So there's no reason you can't tell me."

"There's no reason I should tell you. Curiosity killed the spy."

"It killed the cat," I said.

"The cat happened to be a spy. Cats are sneaky. Haven't you noticed?"

The car rotated, then shot off, forcing me against the

seat. When we reached the end of the ride, we stepped into a lobby a lot smaller than the one in the Museum of Tile and Grout. I followed Mr. Murphy outside. On the way down the steps, I looked back at the building. A small sign over the door read, CIVIL WAR VETERANS' SOCIAL CLUB. I had a feeling they didn't have any members. Unless some soldiers had also been splashed by Hurt-Be-Gone.

Mr. Murphy led me down the street. Two blocks later, I recognized where we were. "It's the Inner Harbor," I said. "We came here on a field trip last year."

Even though it was late, there were a lot of people walking around. Mr. Murphy headed for a bench.

"I want you to stare at people from behind," he said.

"I can do that." I waited until a guy came by. He was eating a slice of pizza and listening to music. As soon as he moved past the bench, I stared at him. He didn't look back. Between the pizza and the headphones, I figured I could have tossed firecrackers at him and he wouldn't have paid any attention. But I did it five more times, with people who weren't distracted by anything. None of them glanced at me.

Mr. Murphy chuckled. "It looks like you really are dead to the world. Now for the real test. Follow the next person. See if you can shadow them for three blocks without being noticed."

That actually sounded like fun. And it was definitely something a spy would do. A guy and a girl strolled past us, holding hands. They looked like college students. This would be easy. They were so busy staring at each other that they wouldn't notice an army marching behind them.

I let them get four or five yards ahead of me before I left the bench. *I am silent. I am invisible.* I pretended I was a ninja slipping through the darkness, wrapped in black clothing and slinking across the pathway like a stalking panther.

Before we even reached the corner, the guy looked over his shoulder and stared at me.

"What do you want, kid?" he asked.

"Uh, nothing." I turned around and scurried back to the bench.

"Not very impressive," Mr. Murphy said. He seemed to be struggling to keep from laughing.

"What's so funny? I thought you said people wouldn't notice me."

"They won't. Unless you act too much like a zombie." He lost the struggle and let out one of his annoying giggles. "You're shuffling your feet."

"No, I'm not."

"Yes, you are." He held his arms straight out in front of himself and swayed from side to side. "You could be auditioning for a cheap horror movie."

"That's not how I walk. Look." I took a couple steps, making sure to lift my feet.

Mr. Murphy turned his right hand palm up. I noticed

he was holding a phone. "Come see how you walked when you were following those people."

After I watched the video, there was no way I could argue with him. I looked like I'd stepped in dog poop with both feet and was trying to scrape it off.

"Let me have another chance. Okay?"

"Certainly. That's why we call it *training*."

An older woman came by, carrying a shopping bag in one hand and a cane in the other. I slipped behind her. This time, I made sure to lift my feet.

It didn't help. She turned around before I'd gone even five steps.

"Back off, sonny boy," she said, raising her cane and jabbing it toward me like a sword. "Or I'll smack you all the way into next week."

"Yes, ma'am." I slunk over to the bench and plopped down next to Mr. Murphy. "I lifted my feet. I know I did. How come she noticed me? Maybe Dr. Cushing was wrong." I felt like I had a giant flashing sign over my head with a big arrow on it pointing right at me.

"You kicked a stone," he said.

"I did?" I definitely hadn't felt it. Though, now that I thought back, I sort of remembered hearing something. This was going to be a problem. I needed to watch my step.

"Try it again," Mr. Murphy said.

We kept at it until it was so late, there was nobody left to follow. I never managed to go more than a block or two before being spotted. I'm not clumsy—Mookie's the one who's always falling over stuff and knocking into things—but I guess, thanks to my numbed senses, I was just awkward enough to keep from being good at following people. I might be okay at noon in a noisy city, but I wasn't going to be following anyone along quiet streets at night.

As Mr. Murphy got up from the bench, he said, "Perhaps stealth is not one of your skills."

"Probably not." I slumped down and put my chin on my hands.

"Don't be so glum, lad," Mr. Murphy said. "There are plenty of other spy skills you can learn. And there are plenty of things you can do that nobody else can accomplish."

"It's not that," I said. I realized something had been on my mind all night.

"What is it?" he asked.

I told him about my doctor's appointment. When I was finished, he said, "Wednesday? Too bad it's so soon. I'm sure, given a little more time, our labs could whip up some devices to help you fool the doctor."

I thought about how all their inventions seemed to explode or catch fire. I could just picture myself in Dr. Scrivella's office with flames shooting out of my ears. "That's okay. I'll get through it."

"I'm sure you will," Mr. Murphy said. He got up from

the bench, and we headed back toward the Civil War Veterans' Social Club.

"Can you tell me anything else about my mission?" I asked.

"Not yet. Just be prepared. We'll probably have to spring into action on short notice. But anything we can do to stop RABID will be worth the effort. Whatever they're planning, I'm sure it's unpleasant."

"I'll be ready."

"Until then, we'll meet each evening to continue your training."

"At BUM headquarters?" I asked.

Mr. Murphy shook his head. "Absolutely not. Patterns are deadly in the spy business. I'll get a message to you."

"Oh, great. Try not to burn my house down. Okay?"

"For a young boy, you really have no sense of adventure," Mr. Murphy said.

I have no sense of lots of stuff.

When we got back to BUM, Dr. Cushing met us. "How'd it go?" she asked.

"Badly," Mr. Murphy said.

"Oh, Peter, don't be so hard on the boy. Give him some time to get used to all of this," she said.

"We don't have the luxury of time," Mr. Murphy said. He walked off.

Dr. Cushing gave me a hug. That took me by surprise,

but it was sort of nice. "Don't feel bad," she said after she'd stepped back. "It's his job to be hard on you. It's also his job to keep you alive."

"Alive?" I asked.

She smiled. "You know what I mean."

"Yeah. Sort of." But I still felt pretty bad.

I took the elevator to East Craven, then walked home. I was skinny enough that I could shimmy up the drainpipe to the garage roof without any trouble. At least I managed to sneak back to my room without being spotted. I stayed there until it was time to get up for school.

I had to be careful not to go downstairs too early. It isn't natural for a kid my age to be awake and alert before the sun comes up. Sometimes, I pretended to be asleep in the morning so Mom could wake me. This morning, even if I had been asleep for real, her scream would have gotten me right out of bed.

5

MP Free

As I ran downstairs, I heard a crash and a second scream. Mom was standing by the kitchen sink, staring at the floor. Her favorite mug—in the shape of a bear with the words STUFFY WUFFY WUVS ITS WORKERS on its belly in pink—was shattered on the floor. A steaming puddle of water spread out from the pieces, flowing around a soggy tea bag and a dark, slimy blotch.

"Are you okay?" I asked.

Mom nodded. "Sorry. I didn't mean to scream. I got startled by this." She shuddered as she pointed at the goop.

"I'll take care of it." I grabbed a handful of sheets

from the paper towel roll and started to mop up the spill.

"Don't get cut!" Mom said.

"I'll be careful."

The blotch looked like the same goop I'd seen in the shower. I told Mom how it had dripped out of the showerhead yesterday.

Mom fanned the air in front of her face and wrinkled her nose. "How can you stand that awful smell?"

Smell? I hadn't even thought about that. I took a small sniff. Ick. It was like a combination of an open sewer on a sunny day and a sweaty T-shirt that had been stuck under a bed for a whole year. And maybe just a touch of cheese.

"You're right," I said. "It's pretty bad."

"That does it." She grabbed the phone book from the top of the fridge. "I'm calling a plumber."

I'd hoped to take another shot at convincing her I didn't need a doctor's appointment, but this didn't seem like a good time for that. It looked like she'd be on the phone for a while. All the plumbers she called were busy. I poured myself some cereal. Mostly, I shook the box and made noise, but I let some flakes fall into the bowl. Then I added milk and went to the table. I hurried through my pretend breakfast, then grabbed my backpack and left for school.

When I got there, I told Abigail and Mookie, "I have a real problem."

"That's awful," Mookie said. "But I bet this will cheer you up. Look what I got!" He held up a white plastic stick about the size of a five-pack of chewing gum. It had a small display screen at the top, and a couple buttons.

I realized he wouldn't listen to my problem until he finished showing us whatever it was he had. "What is it?"

"It's an iClotz. My mom won it," he said. "It's like the most awesome music player ever made. Isn't it cool?"

"Uh, yeah . . ." I tried to sound excited, but I was pretty sure whatever he was holding would turn out to be the opposite of awesome. Mookie's mom was always winning stuff, but it was never the sort of stuff you'd want to win. Last summer, she'd won a year's supply of frozen anchovies. As far as I was concerned, one anchovy was more than a year's supply. And then there was that fried pizza jacket.

"Where are the headphones?" Abigail asked. "I don't see anywhere to plug them in."

"The good ones don't use headphones. This has a miniature speaker system built right in so you can share the music with your friends. Check it out." Mookie shoved it in her face, then held it up to mine.

I could see a bunch of tiny holes in the bottom half, and something round and shiny behind them. "Nice. Real nice. So let's hear it."

"I don't have any music for it yet."

"Can't you download some?" Abigail asked.

"It doesn't exactly work that way," Mookie said.

"So how does it work?" she asked. "Is it wireless? That would be awesome."

"Even better. Watch." Mookie walked over to where Shawna Lanchester and her friends were listening to a radio and dancing. They glared at him, but I don't think he even noticed. He pushed a button on his iClotz, then held it next to the radio. He stayed there for a moment, swaying to the music, then came back.

"Listen to this." He pushed another button.

I heard the same music that was just playing on the radio. "So it records music? That's how you get songs?"

Mookie nodded. "I can put any piece of music in the whole world on it—as long as it's playing somewhere. I can choose from billions of different songs. How cool is that?"

"Just amazing. Do you have anything else you need to show us?" I asked.

"Nope. This is awesome enough all by itself. This is giga-awesome."

"You sure you're all done?"

"Positive," Mookie said. "Did you have something cool to show us, too?"

"I wish." I told them about my appointment with Dr. Scrivella.

"We'll figure something out," Abigail said.

"You mean you'll figure something out," Mookie said. "You come up with all the ideas."

Abigail started to say something, then shrugged and said, "True."

"Hey," Mookie said. "You're supposed to tell me I'm wrong. I have good ideas. Lots of them. I'm the one who figured out Nathan could win money at eating contests."

"And how exactly did that turn out?" I asked him.

"It worked out great," he said. "I got a whole bag of candy. Remember?"

"I'm still trying to forget," I said.

"Face it," Abigail said. "Your ideas don't make things easier for Nathan."

"They will. Maybe I'll even find a cure for him. As a matter of fact, I'm doing important scientific research," Mookie said.

"You? Research? Science?" Abigail snorted. "How?"

I guess the news reduced her to single-word sentences.

"Sure, make fun of me," Mookie said. "But I've been watching every single zombie movie ever made. Even the bad ones. The answers to all of Nathan's problems are in them somewhere."

"That's not science," Abigail said.

Mookie laughed. "That's exactly what they told the Mad Doctor of Zombie Gulch. But he showed them who the real scientist was when he brought all the dead cattle back to life."

"Agh!" Abigail screamed. "I give up!"

"Cool," Mookie said. "That means I win."

"Fine. Great. You win. Let's get back to the problem.

What was your last appointment like?" Abigail asked. "What did the doctor do?"

"The nurse weighed me and measured my height," I said.

"No problem there," she said.

"Then the doctor listened to my lungs and heart," I said.

"Problem," Abigail said. "But a problem is nothing more than an opportunity to be creative. I'm sure I can find a solution."

"That would be excellent." I could picture myself in the examining room. The lung part wouldn't make Dr. Scrivella suspicious. I can breathe when I want to. So I could take a deep breath when he asked me. I'd probably also have to pretend to flinch when he pressed the cold stethoscope against my chest. I think he enjoyed that part. But when he tried to listen to my heart, I'd be in trouble.

"Hey—he'll probably take your temperature and check your pulse, too," Abigail said. "Doctors usually check for a fever before giving a shot."

"Temperature and pulse?" I realized Abigail was right. "That's two more things I don't have. This is awful."

"This is great." Abigail grinned at me. "It looks like I have a lot to figure out. Yay!"

She asked me a bunch of questions, like what kind of thermometer Dr. Scrivella used, and whether he checked my eyes. I guess, for her, having problems to solve was a real treat. She was almost skipping when we headed to home base.

Mookie held up his iClotz again when we reached our classroom. "You don't even need to record a whole bunch of songs, or even a whole song," he said, "because it can repeat stuff."

He put it against my ear, treating me to the same small sample of music over and over until we took our seats.

All morning, Abigail stared at the ceiling. She even got lectured by Ms. Otranto for not paying attention in social studies. She didn't seem to care.

While Abigail was doing her deep thinking, I tested my ability to stare at people without being noticed. I tried it in class and in the halls. It really worked. Nobody turned around. On the way to science class, I gave it the biggest possible test. I got right behind Ferdinand, who is pretty much afraid of everything, and stared at him as hard as I could. He had no idea I was there.

"Stare at Ferdinand," I whispered to Mookie.

"Okay. I'm a great starer." He aimed his gaze at the back of Ferdinand's neck.

Mookie might as well have been firing spitballs. Ferdinand spun toward us and looked around wildly. Fear flashed across his face until he realized it was only Mookie—and not someone like Rodney—behind him.

All through science class, I watched Abigail. It must

be amazing to have a mind like hers. She was the smartest person I'd ever met. Except maybe for Dr. Cushing. And if Abigail was this smart now, I couldn't imagine what she'd be like when she was Dr. Cushing's age.

Abigail didn't let me down. When we were leaving math, which we have right after science in the same room, she spun toward me. "Exothermic reactions!" She grinned like she'd just discovered gold.

"Abracadabra!" Mookie shouted.

I stared at him.

"I thought we were shouting weird stuff," he said. "That seemed like a good choice."

"Not stuff. The solution. This is so perfect." Abigail grabbed my arm. "An exothermic reaction is one that produces heat. Do you see?"

"Maybe . . ." I glanced at Mookie. He was as lost as I was.

Abigail pointed to the closet where Ms. Delambre kept the supplies. "All we have to do is get the proper combination of chemicals that will heat up to a normal body temperature. You mix them in your mouth right before your doctor takes your temperature."

"That sounds dangerous," I said.

"No, it doesn't," Mookie said. "It sounds totally cool."

"It will be perfectly safe," Abigail said. "We're lucky your doctor is old-fashioned. I have no idea what we'd do if he used an ear thermometer."

"Chemicals made me into a zombie," I said.

"These are different chemicals," Abigail said. "Trust me, Nathan. I know what I'm doing."

I looked at the closet. "Can you get some of those chemicals here?"

Abigail shook her head. "I doubt it. They probably don't keep dangerous chemicals around fifth-graders."

"I thought you just told me it wasn't dangerous."

"Not if you're careful," Abigail said. "Look, I can find what I need at the college."

"How are you going to get in there?" I asked.

"I've been helping a couple students with their chemistry homework. And I still have a copy of Uncle Zardo's key. I'll run some tests as soon as we get out of school. Come over after dinner. I should be all set by then."

"I'll come, too," Mookie said. "Just in case something explodes. You'll need me to help pick up the pieces. I'll bring a big trash bag."

"Nothing is going to explode," I said.

But, of course, all through recess, Mookie kept walking behind me and shouting, "Boom!"

Then, he shouted into his iClotz and set it on repeat. "Boom! Boom! Boom!"

"Hey, it's a boom box!" He seemed to think that was especially funny.

Since I'd already come close to blowing up once before, I didn't really share his amusement. He also made it impossible for me to even try practicing following anyone. Add Mookie's clumsiness and his booms to my stumbling, and it was hopeless.

"I'm just a total failure," I told Abigail when we headed in for lunch. "And it's really killing me."

"You need to choose your words more carefully," she said. "But it's not that big a deal. You just had a problem with one thing."

"But it was an important thing. I feel awful."

"I guess I can understand that," she said. "It feels especially bad because you aren't used to failing."

"Are you kidding? I've messed up at all kinds of stuff for as long as I can remember." Some highlights—or maybe they were lowlights—from my life flicked through my brain. I saw sports disasters and social humiliation, along with a bucket full of classroom catastrophes.

"Not since you became a zombie," Abigail said. "Since then, you've been a winner, a hero, and a great student. So one little failure really sticks out. Get over it."

"I'll try," I said. But I was already worried about what Mr. Murphy would ask me to do next. Abigail was right— I wasn't used to failing anymore.

6

Great Gumballs of Fire

"**I brought you** this." Mom handed me a chocolate bar when she got home from work.

"Thanks. I'll eat it later."

"How's your foot?"

"It's totally fine." I wiggled my ankle. "Look, it didn't
rot and fall off."

"Let me see the scratch."

I sat on a chair and pulled off my right sneaker and
sock. Mom knelt down and studied my foot.

"Oh, dear. It doesn't seem to be healing. I'm so glad I
made an appointment with the doctor. This could be a
symptom. I hope you don't have something serious, like

one of those horrible staph infections. Maybe I should take you there right now, even if we don't have an appointment."

"It's fine. Really." She was right, of course. The scratch wasn't healing. But it didn't matter. "I don't even need to see the doctor. It's a waste of time."

I guess I'd pushed too hard. Mom's eyes started to reshape themselves into laser cannons. I braced myself for a blast. Luckily, I was saved by the doorbell.

"That must be the plumber," Mom said.

It definitely was the plumber. Nobody else walks around with a pipe wrench in her belt, dressed in green overalls, carrying a gigantic toolbox. The name SHELLY was stitched over her pocket in gold thread. She had orange fingernails, long hair as nice as Shawna's, and a smile even nicer.

"Mrs. Abercrombie?" she asked. "It's Michelle Stone. You called about gunk in the pipes, right?"

Mom pointed to the kitchen. "It came out of that faucet, and the upstairs shower."

Shelly nodded. "Sorry I'm late. But I've had a lot of emergency calls today. I've been hopping around like a toad on a hot plate. Let's take a look." She headed for the kitchen, then stopped and glanced back over her shoulder toward Mom. "My dad taught me the business. Everybody is curious about that."

She got busy under the sink. I got busy up in my room. About fifteen minutes later, I heard her go into the upstairs bathroom. A bit after that, I heard her tell Mom, "Everything checks out fine, Mrs. Abercrombie. Pipes are clean. Drains are running the way they should. I can't explain it. I wish I could. But if I were you, I'd keep an eye on that willow tree in your front yard. They love water. The roots can go right into your pipes."

She left. I stayed in my room. Mom wasn't going to be happy about the plumbing not getting fixed. But maybe the goop wouldn't show up again.

After dinner, I headed over to Abigail's place, which was just four blocks away on Zackerly Street. She and her mom had finally moved into their house. Mookie was already there, up in Abigail's room.

"Here." I handed her the chocolate bar I'd brought. "My mom got it for me. I guess she felt bad about taking me to the doctor."

"Thanks. Ooooh—with cashews. She must feel really bad." Abigail opened the wrapper and took a bite.

Mookie looked like he was going to ask her to share, but I could see he'd brought two bags of pretzels and a handful of licorice whips with him.

Abigail pulled a bottle and a jar from her backpack and handed them to me. "I think I found everything I needed."

I glanced at the labels. The words on them were really long. "What is this stuff?"

"Just some common chemicals."

"The last time I got near chemicals, they killed me," I said.

"You don't have to worry about that happening again," Mookie said.

"I guess not. But I don't want to do anything else bad to myself."

"I got the most harmless chemicals I could find," Abigail said. "A lot of exothermic reactions involve strong acids or bases. That wouldn't be good. This will be much milder." She fished around in one of the backpack's pockets and pulled out a thermometer.

I watched as she poured a little bit of the powder onto a dish. Then she put a couple drops of the liquid on it. The mixture fizzled and hissed. Abigail held her hand several inches above it and nodded. "Warm." She touched the tip of the thermometer against the mixture, waited for a moment, then said, "Great. This should work beautifully."

"I can't sit there and sprinkle stuff in my mouth," I said. "Dr. Scrivella's eyes aren't that bad."

"I've got it covered," Abigail said. She reached into the backpack again and pulled out a handful of large gumballs.

"Jawbreakers!" Mookie shouted.

He reached out, but Abigail smacked his hand. "This is our delivery system. I'll cut one in half, hollow it out, put the powder in one side, cover it with a small piece of plastic wrap, put the liquid in the other side, then glue the halves back together. All Nathan has to do is bite down on it, and the reaction will start."

"Cool," Mookie said. "That's like the poison pills the spies use." He clamped his jaw shut, twitched violently, then flopped his head over like he'd just swallowed cyanide.

"Will the gumball hold enough of the chemicals?" I asked.

Abigail nodded. "Sure. It will be in an enclosed space. Just keep your lips over the thermometer. We'll run some tests."

Abigail split one of the gumballs with a small kitchen knife and started putting everything together. "Here. Try it," she said when she was done.

I stuck the gumball in my mouth and bit down. A second later, something started foaming out from between my lips.

"Mad dog!" Mookie screamed. "No—it's even worse. Mad zombie!" He waved his hands in the air and ran around the room in circles.

Abigail's mother peeked in right when Mookie banged into a wall. "Oh, I see your friends are here. How nice."

I waited until she left, then spat the crushed gumball in the trash can and wiped my arm on my sleeve.

"Maybe I'll try using a little less this time," Abigail said.

"You think?"

It took three more tries. But she finally figured out

the right amount of the mix so it wouldn't fill my mouth and pour out from between my lips.

"See?" Abigail said as she plucked the thermometer from my mouth and pointed to the display. "You've got a normal temperature. I'll make up three or four of these so you have spares."

"Great." So we had one thing worked out. Maybe I could actually get through my exam, as long as Abigail solved the other problems before tomorrow afternoon. I hoped they were just as easy. "Hey, as long as you're solving problems, how can I hide a scratch from my mom?"

"That's easy. Any girl could figure that one out. Wait right here." She dashed off down the hall.

Any girl? I had a feeling I wasn't going to like this.

Abigail came back a minute later with a small bottle.

"What's that?" I asked.

"Concealer," she said.

"I've never heard of it."

"Me either," Mookie said. "But if it can conceal farts, I want a bottle."

"Nothing could conceal that," Abigail said. She turned to me. "Take off your shoe. Let's see that scratch."

I did what she told me, then waited while she painted some liquid over the scratch and rubbed it with a cotton ball.

"All done." She tossed the cotton ball into the garbage.

I took a look. "Cool. It's like the scratch disappeared. What are you doing with that stuff?"

"It's not mine. I got it from my mom's makeup kit."

"Makeup? . . ." I looked at my foot, then at the bottle. "Don't say anything!" I yelled at Mookie.

But he'd already collapsed on Abigail's floor. Okay, he could go ahead and laugh. If I had to use makeup to hide the fact that my scratches didn't heal, I didn't care.

We hung around a little longer and helped Abigail put up posters. On one wall, Albert Einstein stared across the bedroom at a painting Abigail told me was done by a guy named Monet. The painting was sort of fuzzy, but also kind of cool. I guess you could say the same thing about Einstein. Except for a new computer, Abigail still didn't have a lot of stuff to replace what she'd lost in the fire.

"It must be tough losing so much," I said.

"It's kind of nice not having my closet crammed with things," she said. "It's just stuff. It's not important." She sighed and looked over at her desk. There was a photo there. It was burned at the edges, and stained with water. I guess it had been in the fire. It showed Abigail maybe three or four years ago, in pigtails and a blue dress, with a guy who looked a little like her uncle Zardo, except he didn't have crazy eyes or crazy eyebrows.

"He could help you," she said. "If anyone could find a cure, he could."

"Your dad?"

Abigail nodded. "He could do anything. If he was here, you wouldn't need a fake pulse or temperature. He'd bring you back to life. He'd just go to his lab and not leave until he'd figured out a cure."

"What happened?" I asked. I knew her father had died, but I didn't know how.

I wasn't sure whether she was ready to talk. But after a moment, she said, "He was in Bolivia, studying slime mold."

"Slime mold?" I glanced over at Mookie to make sure he didn't start laughing. But he actually seemed to realize that this wasn't a time for jokes.

"It's a fascinating life-form." Abigail's face lit up as she talked. "Dad taught me all about it. It used to be classified as a fungus, but most scientists have changed their minds about it. Dad was an expert in cell biology. He was pretty awesome with chemistry, too."

"What happened?" I had this horrible image of someone falling into a huge puddle of slime.

"His guides took him down a river. There was an accident with the canoe. That was it. He was gone."

"He'd be proud of you," I said. "You're so smart."

She shrugged. "I don't know."

"Sure he would. You already figured out how to make it look like I have a normal temperature. You're brilliant. That's the truth."

"Thanks." Abigail turned to Mookie. "Mad zombie. That was pretty funny."

"Not as funny as Nate wearing makeup on his foot," Mookie said.

They both started laughing.

"How's your research going?" Abigail asked Mookie.

"Really good. I'm working my way through the alphabet," he said. "I've seen every zombie movie so far from A through Y."

"So you're almost done," I said.

Mookie shook his head. "Nope. I'm about halfway through."

"Oh, right," Abigail said. "Lots of Zs. Was there a movie called *Mad Zombie?*"

"Not yet," Mookie said. "Lots of mad scientists. No mad zombies. Maybe we should make one. We've already got our star." He started laughing again.

When we headed out, Mookie was still laughing. "Mad zombie . . . makeup . . . oh, man—I love hanging out with you. It's always fun."

That night, when I went to brush my teeth, something started to squeeze out of the water faucet. At first, I thought it was one of those globs of goop. I almost called Mom. But it didn't look wet enough. And it wasn't really shiny. I took a sniff. No smell. Then, when about half of it came out, including four legs, I realized it was a spider. A really big spider. It looked like it could eat small birds. I think I would have been happy to see goop instead. I was glad I hadn't touched it.

I stepped back, not sure what to do. I like spiders. I

wasn't going to kill it. But Mom would totally freak out if she saw it. It was so big, I think Dad might freak out, too.

The spider crawled to the top of the faucet and started to spin a web between the sink and the mirror. It worked really fast. I didn't know spiders made webs that quickly. I thought it took hours.

"Oh, great," I muttered when I realized what was going on. Obviously, Mr. Murphy had read too many children's books. The spider was spinning me a message.

7

Some Things Are Hard Pick

The spider had only spelled out "Borloff Lo" when it fell off the web and broke into pieces. I hate to admit it, but I was actually a little disappointed when the pieces didn't explode or burst into flames.

The unfinished message was good enough. I knew where to go. Borloff Lower Elementary. As soon as my parents were asleep, I slipped out to meet Mr. Murphy for my second training session. He was waiting at a picnic table behind the school, with a large suitcase.

"Nice spider," I said.

"Thank you. We just developed it last week."

"I thought it was goop at first."

"Goop?"

I told Mr. Murphy about the gunky sludge in the pipes. I figured he wasn't really interested in my problems, or even in East Craven's problems. Sometimes when I talked to him, it seemed he was just waiting for me to stop so he could tell me the stuff he thought was important. But I noticed he was actually listening to me.

When I was finished, he said, "This could be significant."

"What do you mean?"

"I'm not sure yet." He took a notebook out of his pocket and jotted down a couple sentences. "But let's get to work." He flipped to an empty page, wrote something else, and ripped it out. "A well-rounded spy should have a knack for secret codes. Let's start with an easy one, just for a warm-up."

"Sure. I love codes." My dad had showed me how to use lemon juice to write invisible messages. When you heated the paper with an iron, the message appeared. And way back in second grade, Mookie and I had learned Morse code so we could tap out messages to each other. Except Mookie only learned the code for E, A, T, and S, so his messages were pretty limited to stuff like "Eat."

Mr. Murphy handed the page to me.

I read the message: NTHN BRCRMB. It didn't make any sense. "Northern breadcrumbs?" I guessed.

"Try harder, Nathan," Mr. Murphy said. "This is important."

Maybe each letter stood for another one. I noticed that both words started and ended with the same letter. But that didn't help at all. There were probably millions of words that would fit the pattern.

"Try really hard, *Nathan Abercrombie*," Mr. Murphy said.

Why did he keep mentioning my name? I stared at the page. The letters did look sort of familiar. Oh. Now I saw it. "It's my name without the vowels. Right?"

"Perhaps codes aren't one of your strengths," Mr. Murphy said. "No problem. Let's try something I think you'll be really good at. Ready?"

"Sure." After failing at following and at codes, I was definitely ready to be great at something.

He opened the suitcase. It was filled with locks—padlocks, combination locks, and even some doorknobs with locks on them.

"Don't you usually lock a suitcase from the outside?" I asked.

"Very funny." He lifted one of the padlocks from the suitcase and handed it to me. "A good spy can find a way into any place, no matter how well it's protected. Locks are never a problem. With your steady hands, you should be a natural at this."

"Cool." He was right—I should be really good at this because my hands never shook. I imagined myself breaking into places. I'd slip into the bad guys' hideout and steal their computer files without them even knowing I was there. As long as I didn't have to follow them some-place.

Mr. Murphy held up one of the tools and explained how to use it. Then he handed me the tool and a lock. "Give it a try. Be gentle. You have to feel very carefully for the tumblers when you insert the pick."

Feel? My hands might be really steady—so steady that I was awesome at video games—but feeling stuff was not my best thing. I'd gotten splashed with the Hurt-Be-Gone because I wanted to stop having hurt feelings. Instead, the formula had gotten rid of a lot of my ability to feel actual stuff.

I slid the pick into the keyhole and tried to feel what was going on. Nothing. I moved it around. I wouldn't have done any worse if I were wearing mittens.

"It's no use." I handed the lock and the pick back to Mr. Murphy. "I can't do this."

"Don't give up so quickly. Let's try a combination lock," he said. "Those are easier." He gave me one, and explained what to feel for.

"Forget it," I said. "I won't be able to do it."

"Just try."

I tried. No luck.

Mr. Murphy sighed and started to close the suitcase. Then he paused, reached down, and pulled out a card-board tube. "Let's talk about your doctor's appointment. If the world knows about you, you become much less useful.

You might even be in danger. My people have been working on the problem."

So have mine. I didn't think I should tell him about Abigail—especially right after he mentioned protecting my secret. There was no way he'd understand that the two people I trusted the most in the whole world were fifth-graders. People never believe kids can be as good as adults at things like keeping secrets, solving problems, or saving the planet from evil bad guys.

He pulled a paper from the cardboard tube, unrolled it, and held it up. I looked at the drawing. It was a round plastic ball with a bunch of tubes and wires running out of it.

"What's that?"

"Artificial heart," he said. "It's brilliant. Battery operated."

"Did Dr. Cushing make it?"

He shook his head. "No, this came out of our research department. Dr. Cushing's specialty is medical evaluation."

I pointed at the drawing. "How does it work?" I didn't think I could hide it under my clothing, since Dr. Scrivella would probably ask me to take off my shirt.

"We put it in your chest and run the tubes through your arms to your wrist. Just like that, you have a heartbeat and pulse." He tapped something on the right side of the drawing. "We'll run this wire up your throat to your mouth, and you have a temperature."

"You put it in my chest?"

"Of course."

"How?"

He made a cutting motion with his right hand. "Surgery."

"Are you crazy?" I stepped away. "Nobody is cutting me open."

"Oh stop whining, Nathan. You don't feel pain. And we'll take it right out after the appointment, if you want. Though I suspect it could have other uses if we left it in. Really, this opens up all sorts of possibilities." He paused to giggle, then said, "Opens up . . . that's sort of funny, when you think about it."

"Forget it." I could just imagine the fake heart exploding after they'd sewed it into my chest. That would definitely get Dr. Scrivella's attention.

"Consider the alternative," Mr. Murphy said. "Discovery. Exposure."

"That's all I've been thinking about." I spent half my time hiding who I was and what I'd become. But there was no way I was going to let anyone cut me open and stick stuff inside me. I wasn't a piece of dead meat, and nobody was going to treat me like one.

Pulse Fiction

Once again, **I** headed home after failing my training. It looked like I'd be about as good a spy as I would be a linebacker, or a sumo wrestler. I couldn't do anything real spies did. All I could do was stupid dead-guy stuff. I stared down at my feet as I walked.

Watch your step.

That's what I was always saying to Mookie. Maybe I just needed to take my own advice. I stared at my feet as I walked, being careful how I stepped.

It seemed to work. I walked two blocks without scrapes, scuffs, or accidental sounds. Maybe I could actually follow people. I started to go a third block.

"Ooof!"

I'd walked right into a low tree branch. Okay—that was a problem. If I watched my step, I wouldn't make any sounds, but I'd walk into stuff, and I wouldn't be able to keep an eye on whomever I was following.

An eye . . . That's one eye. I needed to keep one eye on my feet, and one eye on my target. I wondered if I could do both.

I tried looking down with one eye, and ahead with the other. That's when the weirdest thing happened.

Whoa . . .

I could see my feet, and also look ahead. It was like each of my eyes could move by itself, and I could see more at once. Next, I looked toward both sides at the same time, moving my left eye as far left as I could and my right eye as far right. Wow. It was like I could see halfway around me.

Maybe my dead eye muscles worked differently from regular eye muscles. I guess there's something in a living brain that makes both eyes move in the same direction. Whatever the reason, this meant I should be able to follow people. I might still stink at picking locks or breaking codes, but at least I wasn't a total failure.

There wasn't anyone around I could practice on, so I headed home. But when I walked to school the next morning, I managed to follow an older kid for a couple blocks. He finally turned off toward the middle school, but he never noticed me. I'd done it. I felt a lot better as I walked the rest of the way to school.

"Sixty-six point six!" Abigail shouted when I got there.

Instead of saying, *Huh?* I just waited for her to continue.

"Your problem is two-thirds solved," she said. "That's sixty-six point six percent. Actually, point seven if you round up."

"Round 'em up," Mookie said. He swirled his hand over his head like he was twirling a lasso, and went running after imaginary cattle.

I was good enough with fractions to understand what Abigail meant. We had three things to figure out. She'd already solved the temperature problem. So she must have figured out one of the others. "What'd you come up with?"

"This is just incredibly easy," Abigail said. "After you left, I went to the library and did physiology research all evening."

"Fizzy what?" I asked.

"Fizzy!" Mookie yelled as he ran past us. "I love fizzy drinks."

"Not fizzy. Physiology," Abigail told me. "The study of the body. I was looking at the circulatory system—you know, the bloodstream and heart—when it hit me." She held up a small rubber ball, like the kind you buy from gum machines.

"Do you get all your ideas from gum machines?" I asked.

"Well, they are all over the place," she said. "And that's actually where I found this. Right inside the library, next to a machine selling fake tattoos of Edgar Allan Poe and Sylvia Plath."

"What is it?" I asked.

"Your pulse," she said.

"Huh?"

"Put it under your arm," she told me.

Mookie trotted back over to us, panting from his cattle chase. "Ick. That's something Dilby the Digger would do."

"It's something Nathan's going to do if he wants to pass his doctor's exam," Abigail said. She handed me the ball.

I put it under my right arm. Compared with some of the things Abigail had gotten me to do, this was pretty simple. At least I wouldn't end up soaking wet, standing in my underwear, like that time at the aquarium.

"Now what?"

"Press it," she said. "There's a major artery under your armpit. When you squeeze the ball against it, you'll make the blood move. You just need to press and release, and keep doing it while the doctor takes your pulse."

"Are you sure?" I asked.

She grabbed my wrist with two fingers on the top and her thumb underneath—like the way Dr. Scrivella does when he checks my pulse. "Try it. Just do it once. Press and release."

I pressed down on the ball, then let go. "Feel anything?"

She nodded. "Yup. Definite pulse."

That was great. "So, how fast do I do it?"

"Sixty times a minute would be a good rate," she said. "And a convenient one. Use your watch."

I looked at my watch and squeezed the ball in my armpit each time the second hand moved. After a moment, Abigail said, "Perfect. You've got a pulse."

"Thanks. I wish it was that easy to get a real pulse."

Abigail wrapped the rest of her fingers around my wrist. "You will, Nathan. I really believe the process is reversible. Someday, you'll have a pulse and a heartbeat and everything. Somehow. Some way."

"And a sense of smell," Mookie said, flashing me a grin.

"You didn't . . . ," I said.

"Oh no, he did." Abigail pinched her nose and stepped away from Mookie. "Thank goodness we aren't inside."

I didn't care what Mookie did. I was happy I'd have a pulse for my doctor's appointment. "So I have a temperature and a pulse. Now, all I need is a heartbeat."

"Don't worry," Abigail said. "I'll figure that out."

"I hope so. We're pretty much out of time. My appointment is right after school."

73

"I still say you should just get sick," Mookie told me.

"To get out of a doctor's appointment?" I asked. "You want me to tell my mom I can't go to the doctor because I'm sick?" I waited for him to realize the problem with that suggestion, but he just nodded and grinned like he'd invented a way to turn broccoli into ice cream.

He lost his grin at the beginning of lunch. I wasn't eating, of course, but everyone else was diving into their food. Mookie was just about to gulp down his first spoonful of beef barley soup—it's so lumpy, we all called it "barf beefly"—when Abigail grabbed his wrist.

"What's that?" she asked, pointing to his spoon as it hovered a quarter inch from his mouth.

Mookie frowned and moved the spoon far enough away from his face so he could see it. "What's what?"

"That thing," Abigail said.

I saw what she meant. There was a slimy glob of dark green goop sitting in the middle of his spoon.

"Meatball?" Mookie guessed.

"It's not meatball soup," Abigail said. "That looks nasty. I don't think you should eat it."

"It won't hurt me," Mookie said. But, instead of eating it, he took a sniff. "Oh man, maybe you're right. Nothing should smell like that until after it's been eaten. Long after." He dropped the spoon back in his soup and picked up his peanut butter and jelly sandwich in one hand and his burger in the other. "Good thing I bought enough lunch. Where to start?"

"You all better check your soup," Abigail said.

Denali, Ferdinand, and Snail Girl had soup. They fished around with their spoons.

"Mine's fine," Denali said. Even so, she pushed it away.

Snail Girl nodded. I guess hers was fine, too. Ferdinand lifted his spoon, stared at the quivering glob of goop, screamed, flung the spoon away like it was made of hornets, and toppled backwards off his chair.

Naturally, I was sitting right in the path of the spoon and the goop. I got splattered in the face.

"Goop soup," Denali said.

"Super goop soup," Adam Kessler said.

"Hold the slime," Mookie said.

"I can't," Denali said. "It's too slippery."

Around the cafeteria, I could see people at other tables discovering the extra ingredient in their soup. I went to the bathroom to wash my face. When I turned on the water, I halfway expected goop to flow out. But it was just water.

After I'd cleaned up, I went back to my seat and waited for lunch to end. As we were getting up to leave, Abigail grabbed a plastic spoon and scooped up the goop from Mookie's tray. Mookie was usually the last kid to take back his tray, because he had a lot of food to get through. He was always telling the principal that lunch should be ninety minutes. The principal didn't agree.

"Help yourself," Mookie said. "I'm full."

I watched as Abigail pulled a small test tube out of her purse and dropped the goop in there.

"What are you doing?" I asked.

"I want to analyze the sample," she said. She glanced around to make sure the rest of the kids had left. Abigail didn't want anyone in our class to know she was a scientific genius. Girl geniuses get kidded a lot.

"Do you always carry around test tubes?"

"Of course. How else could I gather samples?"

I guess she had a point. "Let me know what you find out."

Mookie and I headed for gym. I was actually happy to go. My mean gym teacher, Mr. Lomux, was still out. Like Rodney, he'd suffered pretty badly during the wrestling disaster. He'd also taken a pretty hard hit to his ego. And since his ego was the largest part of his body, it must have hurt.

The substitute gym teacher showed us how to play shuffleboard. It was pretty cool. You used a stick to slide this puck across the floor. I was actually pretty good at it. But that's not surprising, since my hands are totally steady.

At the end of the day, I checked for one last time with Abigail. She hadn't come up with a solution. I still didn't have a way to fake a heartbeat.

"Thanks for trying," I told her as we walked out of the school.

"I'm sorry I let you down," she said.

"Hey, you did great. You figured out a pulse and temperature. Nobody else could have done that."

"I wish I had a couple more days," she said. "I know I could solve it."

"I know you could, too." But I was out of time. And my secret was about to end up out in the world. *Eek, zombie! Run!* People were going to hate me. This was really going to stink—even worse than the goop in the water.

Mom was waiting for me when I got home from school. She'd taken off early from work to drive me to my appointment.

"I can walk there," I said.

"I like taking you." She handed me another chocolate bar. "What's the matter—is my little man getting too big to go places with his mother?"

"No. It's fine." I was totally out of ideas and excuses. As I followed Mom to the car, I tried to imagine how Dr. Scrivella would react. Maybe he'd be so shocked, he'd pass out. I guess that wouldn't help all that much. Unless he fell, hit his head, and lost his memory.

"Where am I. What happened?" There'd be stars circling his head.

"You just finished examining me. Everything is normal. Here, let me help you fill out my records."

Now I was just being crazy. Nothing was going to save me.

Road Work

I slid into the front seat and buckled up. I really hated the idea that Mom was about to find out her son was dead. Compared with a rusty nail, this was the atom bomb of bad news.

She pulled out of the driveway and drove down our street. Normally, she would have turned left at the corner, but there was an enormous moving van blocking the road to the highway.

"Guess I'll take the river road," she said. "It's longer, but we have plenty of time."

We headed down that way. If I hadn't been so worried about my doctor's appointment, I would have enjoyed the ride. The road follows the Delaware River, winding and snaking along. The houses are mostly up on the hillside because the river floods once in a while. It's a pretty narrow road, so it's like being in one of those video games where you race along and try to force other cars to crash.

Mom doesn't drive like she's playing a video game, of course. She's pretty careful. But she did hit the brakes hard when we came around a curve and saw the guy holding a stop sign. There were a bunch of orange cones along the right side of the road. I could see a bulldozer past them. It was just sitting there.

Mom sighed. I saw her look at the clock on the dashboard, and then over her shoulder, back the way we'd come. "We'll be fine," she said. "We still have half an hour. This won't take long."

I settled back in my seat and put my hand against my chest. *Start beating. Come on. Just for a little while. You can do it.* My heart paid no attention to me. Then I saw something that told me Mom was wrong. A half hour wouldn't be enough. The guy with the sign smiled at me.

I took a closer look at him. He had a fuzzy black beard covering most of his face, and stringy hair hanging out from under his hard hat. But I knew those eyes. And those big ears.

It was Mr. Murphy!

"Looks like we aren't going to make it," I said fifteen

minutes later. I pulled off my shoe and sock. "It doesn't matter. I'm totally healed. See—no scratch."

"Maybe I should turn around," Mom said. She didn't even glance at my foot. "We could still make it."

There was a line of cars behind us. I couldn't see past the curve. But I could hear a honking horn once in a while. The road was too narrow for anyone to safely turn around.

Ten minutes later, Mom got her phone out of her purse and called the doctor's office.

"This is Mrs. Abercrombie. We're stuck in traffic. I'm afraid we'll have to reschedule Nathan's appointment."

No openings, no openings. Come on, give me a break. I tried to force the world to turn my way.

Mom listened and nodded, then said, "That soon? Great. Thank you."

She put the phone back in her purse.

"We're in luck," she said. "They can fit us in tomorrow. Isn't that nice of them?"

"Wonderful."

Up ahead, Mr. Murphy turned the sign around, so it went from STOP to SLOW, and waved us toward the left lane. We moved along. I hadn't really been saved. All I'd gotten was a bit more time. But I was happy BUM cared enough about my problems to try to do something. Of course, I'm pretty sure all the people who'd been stuck waiting for the traffic to move would feel differently.

The good news was that Abigail had an extra day to figure out the problem. I called her as soon as I got home.

"BUM kept my mom from getting me to my appointment," I told her.

"What did they do, blow up the doctor's office?"

"No. They stopped a whole bunch of traffic. I think they dug some holes in the river road, too. But no explosions. Do you think this will give you enough time to get me a heartbeat?"

"I hope so. I tried a couple ideas, but they didn't work."

"They didn't involve cutting me open, did they?"

"Nope. But thanks for the suggestion. I'll add it to the list."

"Add it at the bottom. Okay?" I knew she was kidding, but the idea still creeped me out.

"Nathan, try not to worry. Things will work out. I know they will. By the way, I took that goop sample over to the college and ran some tests on it."

"What did you find out?"

"It's fascinating," she said. "It has all the properties of a by-product of the fungal life process."

"Uh, I might find that more fascinating if I knew what it meant," I told her.

"Sorry. Think of it this way. Every life-form creates waste products."

"Especially Mookie," I said.

"Especially. Anyhow, we go to the bathroom. We

shed skin cells. We exhale carbon dioxide. Fungi have waste products, too."

"So the goop is mushroom poop?" I asked.

"Well, it's not quite as crude as that, but I guess you could put it that way. The weird thing is, it doesn't seem to be the product of any specific fungus I'm familiar with."

We talked a bit more. I learned some other things about fungi. But nothing as amazing as the idea of mushroom poop. I couldn't get the image of a mushroom sitting on a tiny mushroom toilet out of my mind. I didn't share the image with Abigail.

After we finished, I got out the rubber ball, stuck it in my armpit, and practiced my timing for a while. By then, dinner was ready. Mom had decided to make macaroni and cheese. She's the only person I know who makes it crunchy. Not just the top. The whole thing. When Dad called from work, she told him what she was making. Dad decided to work late. I guess he'd rather crunch numbers than macaroni.

That evening, two dozen glowing caterpillars spelled out a message on my window to meet Mr. Murphy down the street at the local park. I couldn't wait to thank him. I just hoped that I didn't completely fail at my training again.

10

Act Natura*lly*

You totally saved me today," I said.

"We have to protect our assets," Mr. Murphy said. "As much as RABID would love to capture anyone from BUM, they'd be especially thrilled to get their hands on someone like you."

"But I have another appointment for tomorrow. My mom's not going to take the river road again. I think she'd drive over a pile of boulders to keep me from missing a second appointment."

"There are other ways to delay things," Mr. Murphy said. "We just need to keep you away from the doctor until Monday. We'll have the heart simulator perfected by then."

"You're not sticking that thing in me," I said. "No way."

"We'll talk about that later," Mr. Murphy said. "Right now, we have some urgent training."

"Urgent?"

He nodded. "We finally got the break we've been waiting for, thanks to you."

"Me? What did I do?"

"When you mentioned that goop in your water, it got me thinking. This is just the sort of thing RABID would be involved in. We did some checking, looked for certain types of activity in the area, and everything started to come together."

"So is RABID in East Craven?" I really hated the idea that they'd come to my town. And I especially hated thinking that they were the ones who'd been messing with the water supply. I'd do whatever it took to get rid of them.

"They're working on creating chaos in East Craven, but their staging base wouldn't be here. They aren't going to set up in the middle of the target area. But they'll be fairly close. I'm pretty sure I know where they are, and I know the identity of the leader of this mission. I have the information we need to infiltrate RABID's staging base."

"Where are they?"

"You'll find out soon enough. For now, nobody knows

but me." He gave me a smug smile. "But let's get back to work. Before we do anything else, we have to be sure you can carry off your role."

"You can count on me." I pictured myself slipping into a secret fortress. But, in the scene, my heroic spy morphed from stealthy secret agent to stumbling zombie, and a hundred bad guys rushed out. Alarms sounded. Security doors clanged shut. I'd failed.

At least it only happened in my mind. I hoped there wouldn't be any locks or codes to deal with.

"What do I have to do?"

Mr. Murphy stood up and pointed at the ground. "Lie down and act dead."

"What?" It's not like I had to act. I was dead—pretty much.

"Trust me—this is crucial for the mission. You need to act totally dead. No talking. No moving. No peeking. Until I tell you to get up, don't move a muscle. No matter what."

That didn't sound anywhere near as cool as slipping into a fortress. But at least it was something I could do. I sprawled out on the ground, letting my whole body flop. I even opened my mouth and let my tongue hang out.

"Nathan," Mr. Murphy said. "This isn't a school play. Stop overacting. Put your tongue back where it belongs, and close your mouth. I asked you to play dead, not stupid."

"Sticks and stones may break my bones," I said.

"Everything breaks your bones. You're as fragile as uncooked pasta. Now please stop being so sensitive, and go back to being dead."

"You aren't very nice."

"Drop dead." At least he said it with a smile.

I closed my eyes.

"Remember," Mr. Murphy said. "Stay that way no matter what."

I heard him walk away. *Now what?* Was I supposed to stay in the park all night? I didn't see how that would get me ready for a spy mission. A moment later, I heard footsteps running toward me. Then I heard a man's voice.

"Hey—are you okay?" Someone shook my shoulder.

Oh, no. The guy thought I was really dead. I opened my eyes, sat up, and started making excuses. "I'm fine. I was playing a game with my friends." I pointed toward some trees. "They're hiding over there. It's a cool game. It's called 'hide and sleep.' Yeah, that's it. They hide. I sleep."

The guy stared at me for a moment, then looked over at Mr. Murphy. "Did you explain things?" he asked.

Mr. Murphy nodded. "I did. I guess I have to explain them again. Perhaps I should use smaller words, though none come to mind." He turned toward me. "Nathan. What part of 'play dead' did you fail to understand?"

"But I thought—"

He held up a hand. "The dead don't think. They don't talk or move, either. Let's try again."

"Okay." I closed my eyes and flopped back down. I'd messed up once, but now I was going to play dead no matter what.

I heard the guy again. "Kid. Hey—are you hurt?" He shook my shoulder. I stayed dead.

I felt hands pressing on my chest. Someone lifted me. I was being carried. I stayed limp and kept my eyes closed. This was easy.

Doors slammed. I heard sirens. We started to move. I had a sudden fear that this was all a trick to take me somewhere and put in the fake heart. It wouldn't even have to be in a hospital. They could slice me open any-where.

I opened one eye a tiny bit to peek around.

"No peeking!" Mr. Murphy said.

I closed my eyes hard.

"Stop scrunching your eyes," Mr. Murphy said.

The van slid around a corner. I felt the cart move. "Whoa." I grabbed the sides.

"Nathan . . . ," Mr. Murphy said.

"Sorry."

We drove for a while longer. I kept as still as I could, but it turned out playing dead is a lot harder than being dead. Finally, I heard Mr. Murphy say, "That's enough for now, Nathan."

I opened my eyes all the way. I wasn't in an ambu-lance. I was in the back of a van, lying on a cart. A small stereo next to me played siren sounds. There were two other people in the van with Mr. Murphy, and a driver up front. I think I'd seen all of them in the hallways at BUM.

I sat up and looked out the window. We were back at the park. "What was that all about?"

"We had to make sure you could remain dead no matter what happened," Mr. Murphy said. "It looks like we'll have to find a different plan."

"No, you won't. I can do this. I just need to practice."

"There's not enough time," Mr. Murphy said. "I'm going to have to figure out some other way to get into RABID's staging base."

"I'm a real fast learner," I said.

Mr. Murphy turned to the van driver. "Go ahead back. I'll walk. I have some things I need to figure out."

He got out. I followed him. Right after that, the van drove off.

"What's so important about playing dead, anyhow?" I asked.

"Sorry—I can't tell you. We work on a need-to-know basis," Mr. Murphy said. "You don't need to know that."

"But—"

"Good night, Nathan."

As he turned away, I said, "Hey—I've been practicing following. I'm getting better at it. I figured out all I really have to do is—"

"Nathan, one thing you need to learn is to accept

your limitations. There are some things you just won't be good at."

"I'm good at following. Really. And I can get good at playing dead. Let me try again."

"Not now. I have to make preparations. This is a disaster." He pulled a phone out of his pocket. "It's my fault for assuming you were ready."

"I thought you didn't trust phones."

"It's an emergency," he said as he slid the phone open. "And this is a secure phone. It has encryption circuitry. It has anti-eavesdropping functionality." He frowned. "Apparently, it also has a dead battery."

At least I could help him there. I reached into my pocket. "Use mine."

"No, thank you." He shook his phone hard.

"That won't help," I said. "It's not a bottle of ketchup."

"Are you an expert on phones?" he asked.

"I'm a kid. That makes me an expert on phones and games." I held up my phone. "See—full battery. Come on, use it."

"What's a fifth-grader doing with his own phone?"

"All the kids have them," I said. Except Mookie. But I wasn't going to start telling him the names of my friends.

"It's not secure," he said.

"But it's an emergency. Right?" I really wanted to help.

He sighed and took the phone. "We need to separate immediately. It's dangerous enough for me to call BUM on this phone. It would be disastrous if we stayed to gether. I'm expendable. You're not. Though I hope you prove to be more valuable in the future. This isn't the Bureau of *Useless* Misadventures."

"I'm not useless."

"We'll see." Mr. Murphy walked away.

I'd totally let him down. He felt I wasn't any good at being a spy. I needed to prove he was wrong.

I decided to follow him.

11

Follow the Leader

I waited until Mr. Murphy was half a block ahead of me. Then, with one eye on my feet and one eye on his back, I started following him. If I could trail a master spy without being noticed, that would prove how good I was.

He talked on the phone as he walked, trying to assemble a team to go after RABID. Even though he kept his voice low, I could hear most of it. That was another of my zombie skills. Living people have blood rushing through their heads, making noise. I don't, so I can hear better. He never looked back. He never even slowed down.

This was great. After six blocks, I decided I'd sneak up right behind him and then shout, "Boo!" That way, he'd always remember I had awesome following skills. And it would be sort of fun to make him jump. He acted like he was the coolest guy in the world, and that I was nothing but a kid who had to be told what to do. After this, he'd have to respect me.

I sped up, but still kept an eye on where I was stepping. We were only two blocks from the museum. Mr. Murphy closed the phone and put it in his pocket. A second later, I saw a van cruising down the street. It wasn't the same one from before. That one had been green. This one was black. It pulled up next to Mr. Murphy. Maybe he was getting a ride.

I guess I wouldn't have a chance to sneak up and startle him. But I could still run over and prove that I was good at following. We'd gone all those blocks without him noticing me.

Before I could move, the door slid open. Mr. Murphy spun around. Two men leaped out and grabbed him. They dragged him to the van and tossed him inside. Then they jumped in and slammed the door.

I realized I'd just seen Mr. Murphy get kidnapped right in front of me. Maybe RABID had found him before he was able to find them. I tried to read the license plate. It was splattered with mud.

I had to tell someone from BUM. I ran to the Museum of Tile and Grout. The door was locked. I rattled it. If only I'd learned how to pick locks, I could have gotten in. But I'd failed at all my spy lessons. There was no way I was getting inside the museum tonight.

There had to be some way to get a message to BUM. Even if I had my phone, I didn't have a number for them. I ran home and went to the computer. The first time Mr. Murphy contacted me, it had been while I was playing *Vampyre Stalker*. I logged in and looked around for Peter Plowshare—that's the player name he used. He was there, right where I'd last seen him. But he was just standing with his head bowed down. That meant nobody was playing him right now.

It didn't matter. I still had to try to get through. I started typing a message in the text box. "P.M. has been captured. I don't know what to do." I hit ENTER.

There was no reply.

I thought about calling the police. Maybe I'd do that if I couldn't get into BUM tomorrow. They had to be open during the day. Someone there would know what to do.

I got dressed earlier than usual. Even so, Dad was already gone. "I have to get to school for a project," I told Mom as soon as she came downstairs. I had a bowl in front of me with a splash of milk and a few soggy pieces of cereal. "I got breakfast for myself."

"Do you want a ride?" Mom asked.

"No, thanks." I grabbed my backpack, then headed out. But instead of walking to school, I ran to the museum and yanked on the door handle.

The door wasn't locked. I almost fell on my butt as it pulled open.

The place was empty. Really empty.

There was nothing inside. No furniture. No paintings on the wall. Even the carpet was gone. It was like someone had removed all signs that BUM ever existed. I walked over to the elevator door. It didn't open. There wasn't any button to press.

There was nothing left for me to do here. This was a dead end.

12

Say Aha!

I left the museum and headed to school. I couldn't believe how quickly everything had gone from fun spy games to total disaster. Maybe I was better off without BUM. But someone had to stop RABID from messing with my town.

After I told Abigail about Mr. Murphy, she said, "There's nothing you can do about that right now. Let's deal with one thing at a time. There has to be some way to mimic a heartbeat."

"I hope so. I really don't want to end up on the front cover of some sort of magazine for doctors." I could just see Dr. Scrivella trying to listen to my heart. I wondered how long he'd search for a beat before he realized something was wrong.

I looked over at Mookie. He was shouting into his iClotz. "Mook-Mook-Mookie! Mookie-Mookie-Moo!" Then he hit the switch, and his voice played back. He looped it and cranked the volume up and down. "Just call me DJ MookieMook."

"Will you stop that!" Abigail yelled at him. "It is so annoying, I can't think."

"You're just saying that because you don't have one," Mookie said. Then he pushed the RECORD button again and said, "Abigail, Blabigail."

"That's so obnoxious," she said. "That's—" Then her eyes went wide. "—the answer!"

"What?" I asked.

"It's so simple. Why didn't I see it before?"

"See what?" I asked.

"We'll record a heartbeat," she said. "I'll rig up a stethoscope and make the recording. Then you can swallow the player. When your doctor listens to your chest, he'll hear the heartbeat."

"Swallow the player?" Mookie and I both shouted.

"Sure," Abigail said. "Don't worry. We'll tie it to a string around one of your teeth, and lower it to the right spot. You can swallow it before you go into the examining room. Just set the playback so it repeats."

She snatched the player out of Mookie's hands.

"Hey—that's mine," he said.

"Nathan needs it more than you," Abigail told him.

He looked like he was going to complain, but then he shrugged, grabbed the ends of his jacket, and ran around playing MookieHawk.

I felt the gumballs in my pocket, and the rubber ball. Temperature and pulse. Add in a heartbeat, and I was as good as alive. Maybe I could get through my exam. "Thanks," I said. "This is great."

"You don't look very happy."

"I was supposed to have an important mission—a real spy mission. Now, it's not going to happen. Who knows what the bad guys will be able to do? Mr. Murphy thinks they're behind the goop in the water."

"Maybe it can still happen," Abigail said. "What do you know?"

"I don't know anything," I said. "Just that I was supposed to play dead." As the words left my lips, I realized they wouldn't be able to resist making smart comments.

Abigail nodded and said, "That would definitely be within your current skill set."

Mookie laughed as he ran around us in a circle. "Wow, that's like asking me to play hungry."

"But it doesn't tell us anything," I said.

"It tells us a lot," Abigail said.

"Like what?"

"I'm not sure yet," she said.

"You know what's really funny?" Mookie asked.

"What?"

"You have to act dead for BUM and alive for your doctor."

"If it was the other way around, things would be perfect," I said. But at least I had a chance to fool my doctor.

"**No goop in** the soup," Mookie said at lunch. He lifted his spoon to show nothing but little pieces of sausage.

"That's even more disgusting," Denali said.

"How could you even take a chance?" Ferdinand asked. "There could have been goop in it."

"I like soup," Mookie said.

"Last night, when we were washing our dog, some goop came out of the faucet," Denali said.

"I saw some right before I went to bed," Ferdinand said. "I'm not ever going to shower again. I'm not even going to drink water anymore."

"It's definitely a problem," Adam said.

"It's nothing to worry about," Denali said. "I'm actually happy about it, because it stains clothing."

I could understand why she felt that way. Her parents had a dry-cleaning shop. I wasn't sure how I felt. The goop was nasty and stinky, but there didn't seem to be a lot of it. Besides, unlike Ferdinand, I really could stay away from water.

o o o

By the end of the day, Abigail had whipped up a stethoscope from parts she found around the school, and recorded Mookie's heartbeat. Since I once saw her make a telescope out of two lenses and a cardboard tube, I didn't even bother asking her how she rigged up a stethoscope. I was just happy to have a heartbeat on the iClotz. Abigail had done her job. The rest was up to me.

That afternoon, Mom gave me an even bigger chocolate bar—Abigail would be happy about that—and drove me to my appointment. We got there without any trouble. I guess with Mr. Murphy kidnapped, nobody had made plans to stop my appointment.

I waited until the nurse put me in the examining room, then swallowed the iClotz. That was definitely one of the weirder things I'd done recently. It dangled from a tooth on a piece of fishing line. I also took one of Abigail's gumballs from my pocket and popped it in my mouth.

Dr. Scrivella smiled at me when he walked into the exam room. "Well, there, Nathan. You've certainly grown into a strapping young lad. I remember when you were a wheezy little baby. Let's see how you're doing."

I showed him my right foot. "I had a scratch, but it's all healed. My mom was worried. You know how moms get."

He laughed. "Moms keep me in business." He squinted at my foot for a moment then nodded. "The foot is fine. Let's see if you've got a fever."

I wish.

He opened a drawer and pulled out a thermometer. I got ready to bite down on the gumball. But the thermometer wasn't the kind you stick in your mouth. It was the kind you put in your ear. Mom had one like that. I'd always hated the way it felt when she jammed it in my ear. I thought about crushing the gumball in my hand and squirting some of the mixture in my ear. But I was afraid what would happen if the reaction went off in such a small place. I might get a bunch of foam shooting out of my ear. Or I might blow my ear off. Even if I could glue it back, it would be hard to find all the pieces. And even harder to explain things to Dr. Scrivella.

If I let him stick that thermometer in my ear, it was all over. It's definitely not cool to have no temperature.

13

☠

Stuff Gets in the Way

I had to do something. Dr. Scrivella squinted as he aimed the end of the thermometer toward my ear. The instant he stuck it inside, I let out a loud laugh and jerked away.

"Easy there, Nathan. This won't hurt." He started to insert the thermometer again.

I jerked away again. "That tickles!"

He stared down at the thermometer. "You're right. I hate this new-fangled stuff. The old-fashioned way is always the best." He reached into the drawer and pulled out a mouth thermometer. By the time he got back to me, I'd crushed the gumball.

I could actually feel a bit of tingling as the liquid flowed under my tongue.

"Open up."

I opened my mouth a bit.

"No jumping," Dr. Scrivella said.

I nodded. He put the thermometer in my mouth. I sealed my lips around it. I could feel my cheeks puffing a bit. The reaction was definitely working.

A moment later, Dr. Scrivella pulled out the thermometer, looked at it, and nodded. "You're definitely normal," he said. "But that's a good thing."

He wrote something down on a sheet of paper in my file. Then he gave me a shot. I pretended it hurt.

"All right. Give me your wrist."

I started to hold my hand out. "Achooo!" I faked a sneeze. As I bent over, I slipped the rubber ball under my arm and clamped it down in my armpit.

Dr. Scrivella took my wrist and felt for my pulse. But instead of looking at his own watch, he grabbed my other arm and turned my watch toward himself. I guess he thought that would amuse me. I wanted to yank my arm away, but that would make him suspicious.

Calm down. You can do this.

There was a clock on the wall, but it didn't have a second hand. Dr. Scrivella was feeling around on my wrist and frowning. I had to act right away. I'd practiced so much, I was pretty sure I could keep up the right rhythm without looking at my watch.

I kept up the squeezing until he nodded and dropped his hand from my wrist. "Sixty," he said. He smiled at me and added, "Like clockwork. You could get a job in a watch factory."

"Thanks."

"All right. Take off your shirt. Let's have a listen to the ticker."

I sneaked the ball back into my pants pocket as I was slipping off my shirt. Dr. Scrivella put his stethoscope against my chest. I didn't feel anything, but I flinched to make him think I did. He listened for a moment, frowned, then said, "A little sluggish. I suspect you haven't been getting enough exercise."

I realized he'd been listening to Mookie's heart. "Yeah. I guess I've been playing too many video games. I'll try to do better."

He slapped my knee. "Good lad. Exercise is the key to living longer. That and good nutrition."

"I'll try to remember that."

"Deep breath," he said, putting the stethoscope against my back.

"Excellent," he said a moment later. "Your lungs sound really good."

And that was it. Thanks to Abigail, I'd survived a doctor's exam without anyone finding out that I was dead. I put my shirt back on and hopped off the examining table. "See you in a year," Dr. Scrivella said.

"I hope so."

I headed out to the waiting room. Mom was on her cell phone. She looked distracted.

"Do you mind walking home?" she asked.

"What's wrong?"

"They called me from work. Stuffy Wuffy is mobbed. Seventeen people just showed up asking to make bears. They need me."

That was weird. I had a hard time believing there were seventeen people in all of New Jersey who'd want to stuff their own teddy bear. "No problem. I can walk."

"I could call your dad," she said. "But he's still at work."

"Really, it's no problem." A walk would give me a chance to think. I was worried about Mr. Murphy, but there wasn't anything I could do to help him right now.

Mom drove off, and I headed home. I hadn't gone more than half a block when a car pulled up next to the curb. The window rolled down. Maybe the bad guys had tracked me here somehow. I got ready to run.

"Nathan, get in."

It was Dr. Cushing. "Boy, am I glad to see you." I opened the door and got in.

"I'm glad to see you, too, Nathan."

"Mr. Murphy was kidnapped," I said. "I'm totally freaked out."

"We know. We were afraid you'd be spooked. But we needed to talk with you. That's why they sent me instead of someone you didn't know. And that's why we just sent seventeen people to the mall to buy teddy bears. We need to figure this out, and we need to do it quickly. I'm afraid we're almost out of time. Based on our experience, we're pretty sure RABID isn't going to risk keeping Peter around for more than twenty-four hours."

"But they grabbed Mr. Murphy last night—so we only have . . ."

"Two or three hours," she said.

"How come BUM was cleared out?" I asked.

"We only cleared out the entry point near where Peter was captured. He'd never reveal the other locations, no matter what they did to him, but we couldn't take a chance in case this one was compromised."

"Are those people really that bad?"

"Worse. I know it's hard to accept if you haven't been exposed to that sort of organization. But they will do whatever they can to destroy our freedom."

"So we have to stop them. Do you have any idea where they are?"

She shook her head. "Peter figured it out. He's brilliant at that sort of thing. But he didn't tell anyone—not even the strike team he was trying to assemble. All they knew was that the target would be less than fifty miles from here. That's one of our problems. We keep things far too secret—even from each other."

"So it's hopeless," I said. But it couldn't be. We had to rescue Mr. Murphy.

"Did he say anything to you last night?" Dr. Cushing asked.

I thought back. "He had me play dead. He said it was crucial to the mission."

"Play dead?" Dr. Cushing stared up at the sky and tugged at the ends of her hair. She really reminded me of Abigail now. "If you were found dead, they'd take you to a hospital. But that doesn't make sense. Why would he want to get you into a hospital?"

"We could go to the nearest hospital," I said.

"But if we're wrong, it will be too late. Peter doesn't have much time. We can't afford a mistake. And we still don't know exactly what sort of disaster RABID is planning."

I knew what I had to say, but I thought for a long time before I spoke. "I have a friend who can help," I said. "She can figure out anything. But I don't want her getting all mixed up with spy stuff. I don't want her in any danger. So you have to promise me you won't tell anyone else at BUM about her."

Dr. Cushing stared at me for a moment. I guess she was weighing everything in her mind. Finally she nodded and said, "I promise."

"Okay. Let's go." I gave her directions to Abigail's house.

14

Of Corpse

Luckily, **Abigail was** home. And, luckily, her mom was out, so I didn't have to explain why I was bringing a stranger with me. Mookie was there, too. I don't know whether that was lucky or unlucky.

I introduced everyone, then told Abigail the problem. She pounced right on it. "The bad guys have to be someplace where people would bring a dead kid. But a regular hospital isn't a good place for bad guys to set up headquarters." She went to the living room and turned on her computer. "So maybe we need to find a hospital that is in transition, or is adjacent to a location that would be suitable for a covert operation."

"Good thinking," Dr. Cushing said.

"I'm glad she understood that," Mookie said. "I sure didn't."

Dr. Cushing leaned over Abigail's shoulder. "You could check public records."

"Absolutely," Abigail said. "But any change in a hospital would be news, so I could scan news sources first, as long as I use the right keyword."

"Try transition, repurpose, downscale, or obsolete," Dr. Cushing said.

"Excellent idea," Abigail said. "I'll limit the range to regional sources." She was almost glowing. I guess the thing she needed most was someone who totally understood her.

They kept talking like this while Abigail typed. Mookie and I looked at each other.

"How come I never know what's going on?" he asked.

"Same reason I don't, I guess."

Ten minutes later, Abigail said, "It's not a hospital. Nothing we found fits."

"Which means it has to be somewhere else," Dr. Cushing said. "But where?"

"Hey," Mookie said. "In the zombie movies, they're always taking the bodies to the local funeral home. Then, the zombies pop off the tables in some creepy old basement and everyone runs away screaming." He held out his arms and lurched around the room.

Abigail and Dr. Cushing both stared at Mookie for a

moment. I was about to tell him to stop distracting them when they both shouted, "Brilliant!"

Mookie staggered back like he'd been smacked on the head. "Really?"

They both nodded.

He grinned.

"In some towns, especially small ones, a funeral director has the job of coroner," Dr. Cushing said. "They'd take the body there. We just need to figure out the most likely person." She pulled out her phone. Unlike Mr. Murphy, Dr. Cushing obviously kept her battery charged.

"You have a database of suspicious persons, right?" Abigail asked.

Dr. Cushing nodded. Then she started talking on the phone. "We have a lead. I need you to screen our watch lists for anyone who works at, or owns, a funeral home." She waited a moment, listened, then told us, "There are five hits, but only one within fifty miles of here."

"That has to be it," Abigail said.

"I hope so," Dr. Cushing said. She put her phone away, grabbed a piece of paper, wrote down some information, then turned toward us. "There's a small town in Delaware, just over the border. Dobbsville. The local coroner is also the funeral director."

"If you know where it is, why can't you just rush in?" I asked. "Or call the police?"

"They'd kill Peter," she said. "And they'd destroy their computer files. We wouldn't get anything. We need someone who can slip in there undetected and set Peter free. Maybe even reach the computers, though that's no longer a priority. It has to be you, Nathan."

"Let's do it," I said.

Dr. Cushing picked up her phone again. "I'll call a couple field agents to take you there."

"No," I said. "I want you to take me."

Dr. Cushing looked like she was going to argue, but finally she nodded.

"You'd better phone home," Abigail said.

I reached in my pocket, then remembered that Mr. Murphy had my phone. Which was another reason I'd risk just about anything to rescue him.

"Here, use mine," Abigail said. She tossed her phone to me, but it went too high and landed behind her bed. "Oops. Sorry. Just put it on my desk when you're done. Mookie and I have to go do more research at the library."

"We do?" Mookie asked.

"Yes, we do." Abigail grabbed his arm and dragged him off.

"She seemed to be in a hurry," Dr. Cushing said.

"I'm sure she had a good reason." I crawled under Abigail's bed, found her phone, then called home and left a message saying I was having dinner with Mookie.

After I put the phone on the desk, Dr. Cushing and I

left Abigail's house and drove off toward Delaware. It was time for me to play dead. I just hoped I was getting there soon enough to keep Mr. Murphy from playing dead for real.

15

From Two to Four

Dr. Cushing drives a lot faster than either of my parents. Maybe faster than both of them combined. As fast as she was going, I had the feeling the car wasn't anywhere near its top speed. It seemed pretty powerful. Dad would have loved it.

"Is this your car?" I ran my hand along the side of the seat. It felt like real leather.

"I wish. BUM keeps a variety of vehicles near all our entry points."

She nudged the gas a bit more. We flew past the other cars on the road. She was definitely over the speed limit. But we had a long way to go, and a life to save.

Right after we got out of East Craven, I heard sirens. An unmarked state police car shot up behind us. Dr. Cushing didn't slow down or pull over. Instead, she reached toward the dashboard and opened a compartment above the radio. I saw five buttons there.

"That's not for smoke screens or that kind of stuff, is it?" I guess I'd been playing too many computer games.

She flashed me a smile. "Press the one that says, 'Authorize.'"

I pushed it. A moment later, the siren stopped and the police car dropped back.

"What happened?" I asked.

"You just sent their in-car computer a message authorizing us to do whatever we need to do to get where we're going."

"That's cool," I said.

"There are some benefits to helping the government." She floored the accelerator, then said, "Nervous?"

"Nope, I like going fast."

"I mean, about your mission?"

"Just in here," I said, tapping my head. "Not down here." I pointed at my gut.

"That makes sense. Your autonomous nervous system doesn't work."

"Autonomous?"

"The automatic stuff. Heartbeat. Respiration. All those organs that squirt chemicals into your bloodstream. When living people come face-to-face with danger, our bodies get us ready to fight or flee. Your body doesn't do that. So, no feeling of panic. No rush of adrenaline. That's good for a spy."

"I guess. This is my first real spy mission."

"Mine, too," she said as she slid through a sharp curve.

"What?"

"I told you, I'm not an agent. I'm a doctor. I work in a lab. They don't train us to do spy stuff. But don't worry. We'll be fine. I have the easy part. All I have to do is get you there in one piece."

I guess I did have the hard part. I didn't have a clue what I'd need to do once I got inside the funeral home. "Do you know anything about the bad guy?"

Dr. Cushing nodded. "They downloaded his file to my phone. You can check it out."

"Mr. Murphy doesn't like using cell phones," I said.

"Secure phones are fine," Dr. Cushing said.

I took the phone and read the file. It was amazing how much information there was. They even had pictures. The guy who owned the funeral home, Gregor Smetchinski, had come here from Russia twenty years ago. But he'd made five trips to the Middle East in the past three years, and one trip to Eastern Europe. He was suspected of involvement in several of RABID's messier plots, but there was no solid evidence. Still, his actions were suspicious enough to put his name in BUM's computer. I finished reading, then put the phone down.

A couple minutes later, Dr. Cushing sniffed the air.

"Good grief—that's awful. What is it? Do they slaughter pigs somewhere around here?"

Since I don't breathe, I never smell stuff unless I make myself take a breath. I sniffed. Oh, no. It wasn't just sickening—it was also familiar. "Pull over."

"What's wrong?"

"Just pull over and pop the trunk."

As soon as Dr. Cushing pulled to the shoulder, I got out and went behind the car. Sure enough, Mookie and Abigail were in the trunk. Mookie was grinning. Abigail was holding her nose and quivering like she was trying not to throw up.

Dr. Cushing joined me. "This is not good."

"I guess I blew my cover," Mookie said.

"Cover?" Abigail screamed. "It smells like you blew out your intestines. We need to flush your entire digestive system with a fire hose."

"What are you doing here?" I asked.

"We figured you might need our help," Mookie said. "So we sneaked into the trunk." He held out a bag. "Want a pretzel?"

Dr. Cushing looked over her shoulder toward East Craven. "There's no time to go back. Get in."

She waited until they'd climbed into the backseat, then got in the car and pulled on to the road. Twenty minutes later, we reached Dobbsville.

"Come on," Dr. Cushing said. "Let's find a good place for you to die."

16

☠

The Zombie Accident

We drove off the highway and searched for a road that had some traffic, but not so many cars that we couldn't set things up.

"This looks good," Dr. Cushing said as we cruised past a street that was five blocks and two turns away from the main road.

Just as we were pulling over to the curb, her cell phone rang. She answered it, spoke for a moment, then turned to me. "They've tried to find out as much as they could about the staging base. The only thing we've learned is that satellite photos show some evidence of construction next to the funeral parlor. But there's nothing on the surface. So the staging base might be underground."

I might end up underground, too, if I messed up at the funeral parlor. But at least I knew a little bit more about what I was going to face when I got there. "Anything else?"

Dr. Cushing handed me a flash drive. It was twice as thick as the normal ones and had a small antenna attached to it. "This has an auto-run copy program, and a transmitter."

"Will it explode?"

She flashed me a grin. "No. It's not from our research department. It's from the computer store."

I was glad the question made her smile. "What do I do with it?"

"If you get a chance, plug it into any port on their computer, and you're all set. It will copy the files and send them to BUM. But don't take risks. Smetchinski is probably extremely dangerous and ruthless. I wish we didn't have to send you in."

"I'll be fine." I looked at the road in front of the car. "So, should I just fall down and act dead?" It sounded simple. But it hadn't been that easy the last time I'd tried.

"A bicycle accident would look more convincing," Abigail said.

"If we had a bike," I said.

She pointed to the trunk. "We do."

Dr. Cushing popped the trunk again. I looked inside.

Sure enough, there was an old two-wheeler pushed in the back.

"I'm impressed," Dr. Cushing said as she pulled the bicycle from the trunk.

"I thought you didn't have a bike," I said. The last time I'd seen her on one, she'd borrowed it. And, to tell the truth, watching her ride was actually one of the scarier experiences I've had in a while.

"I was such a bad rider, I figured I'd better practice," Abigail said. "So I bought one with some of the money I made tutoring."

Dr. Cushing started to close the trunk, but Abigail stopped her and reached back in. "We need one more thing." She pulled out a bike helmet. It was split in half.

"What's that for?" I asked.

"It will help convince them that this was an accident," she said. "Put it by the lamppost. That way, they won't treat it like a crime scene. We don't want anything to delay your trip to the funeral home."

I took the two parts. "How'd you break it?"

"Learning to ride," she said.

Dr. Cushing put the bike on its wheels and rolled it over to me. It wobbled a bit, like it had been in more than a few collisions already. "I guess the rest is up to you, Nathan. We'll go around the corner, out of sight, and wait until they take you away. Then I'll park near the funeral home. If you think you're in danger at any point, just get away however you can."

"I'm not leaving without Mr. Murphy," I said.

"Good luck," Abigail said.

"This is awesome," Mookie said.

I hoped he was right. I was about to do a whole bunch of things I'd never planned on. I watched Dr. Cushing drive off. This wasn't a game. This was for real.

Ready to be a spy?

Yeah. I was ready.

I waited for the street to clear, walked to the curb, and let the bike fall. I thought about stomping on one of the wheels to make the accident look even more realistic, but I was afraid I'd break my foot.

"Here goes . . . ," I said. Dead kid playing dead. How weird was that? I hoped I could do a better job of playing dead this time. I had to. There was no other choice.

I put half the helmet right next to me and tossed the other half onto the sidewalk. I sprawled out on the ground, facedown with my eyes closed, near a lamppost. Then I waited.

It didn't take long.

I heard tires screech. Then I heard car doors.

"Hey, kid," a man said. He shook my shoulder. I stayed limp. "Kid? You okay? Wake up."

I managed to keep from answering him.

"Don't move him," a woman said. "He could be hurt."

"I think he's more than hurt," the man whispered.

The woman started to cry. It took all my strength not to open my eyes and tell her I was okay.

119

A minute later, I heard a siren.

Then things got real busy. People tried to get me to answer them. I stayed dead.

"Unresponsive," someone said.

Somebody rolled me over onto my back. I felt someone pressing my chest. They slipped some sort of mask over my nose and mouth, and something else around my neck. Someone pumped air into my lungs. It all felt totally weird, but I managed to keep my eyes closed.

I heard my shirt being ripped. They did something to my pants, too.

They lifted me.

I was being carried. It sounded like they were putting me in an ambulance.

Doors slammed.

Seconds later, we raced off with the siren blaring. The one thing that kept me playing dead was the thought of Mr. Murphy being held by RABID. I had to save him.

All through the ride, and after we got to the hospital, the paramedics and doctors really tried to bring me back to life. It felt good to know they worked so hard, though nothing they did could possibly make a difference. I guess I felt a bit bad about tricking them. But when you're a spy, sometimes you have to trick people.

Finally, they rolled the cart I was on back outside. They lifted me up again. I heard the ambulance doors close. This time, there wasn't any siren. No high-speed drive. No hurry. Ten minutes later, they rolled me out. It felt like I was being carried down some steps. Then they picked me off the cart and put me on another flat surface. Probably a table.

They walked away. I heard a door close. Through my eyelids, I could tell they'd shut off a light. And then there was silence.

I guess I was where I needed to be. I didn't want to open my eyes, but I had to. I was afraid I'd find myself surrounded by bodies.

It wasn't as bad as I thought it would be. Just a dimly lit room with five tables. Empty tables, except for me. I was glad about that. The walls were unpainted brick. There were three steel poles under a beam in the center of the room. I guess I was in a basement. Like in the zombie movies Mookie told me about. I looked down.

My shirt was gone.

So were my pants.

I was in my underwear.

At least I wasn't wet.

I saw two doors. One led to a hallway. The other, behind me, was solid. That had to lead to the bad guys. The table wiggled a little and creaked as I slipped off it.

I walked over to the solid door and tried the knob. It was locked. There was a keyhole in the knob. Even if I'd learned how to pick locks, I didn't have any sort of pick with me.

A door closed at the other end of the hallway. I heard footsteps. Someone was coming.

17

Breaking In

I **scooted back** to the table and stretched out again. But I kept my eyes open. I wanted to see what was going on. I figured I'd look just as dead if I stared straight ahead.

A guy came through the door, carrying a take-out bag from a burger place. He barely glanced at me, but I recognized him from the pictures on Dr. Cushing's phone. It was Gregor Smetchinski.

"Stupid kid," he muttered. "You must have messed up."

I guess he was used to seeing bodies down here. He reached in his pocket and pulled out a key ring. "You're better off missing what's coming."

I didn't like the sound of that. But I could worry about it later. Right now, I had to figure out how to get through that door. Abigail would have invented a clever plan. But Abigail wasn't here. And there was no time to think. I didn't have a clever plan, but I had a wild one. I guess wild would have to be good enough.

I acted. But I acted in a very small way. I waited until Smetchinski put the key in the lock, then wriggled my body. Just once—and just enough to get a tiny creak out of the table.

He froze, then pulled the key from the lock and walked to the table. He leaned over and stared right into my eyes. Even though his face was so close that I could see the tiny red veins in his eyes, I stayed still. After a moment, he went back toward the door.

I wriggled again when he put the key in.

Once again, he pulled out the key and walked back toward me.

Once again, I remained dead.

This time, I waited until he actually unlocked the door.

Wriggle. Creak.

He dropped his hand and turned toward me.

I sat up, screaming like the living dead coming back to life. "Gaaaaaaaahhhhhhhh!!!"

I howled again and thrust my arms in front of me, then slid off the table, landing on my feet.

"Brains!" I screamed, like I had the biggest craving

in the world, and I'd be happy to bite into his skull to satisfy it. I took a staggering step toward Smetchinski. "Must eat brains!"

His eyes got so wide, I thought they'd fall to the floor. He opened his mouth to scream. Only a thin whine came out, like a balloon losing air. I'd heard about people being too scared to scream, but I always thought it was just an expression.

I took another step. "Kill! Kill!"

Maybe people who work with the dead are especially scared by them when they seem to pop back to life. He dropped the bag and leaped toward the door to the hallway. I heard a loud WHACK! as he ran right into a pole. He went down hard. I could tell from all the way across the room that he'd be out for a while.

Who needs to pick locks? Not me.

"Nighty-night," I said as I walked over to the door and took the keys from the lock. I'd hoped to scare Smetchinski off long enough so I could rush in and rescue Mr. Murphy. It looked like I'd have a bit more time than that.

It's hard to think like a spy when you're only wearing underwear. There was a plastic bag on the counter near the tables. I found my clothes in it. The shirt was ripped. The pants legs were slit halfway up. My jacket was missing. Mom was going to kill me. I put on the pants, then went back to the door.

I checked my pockets. I had the iClotz, a rubber ball,

a couple of Abigail's gumballs, the flash drive Dr. Cushing gave me, and a bottle of the bone glue I always carried. Not exactly what I'd ask for if I was collecting spy supplies. I dropped the keys in my pocket, just in case Mr. Murphy was locked up.

Still trying to think like a spy, I went back over to the guy and checked his pockets. There was nothing in them except for a slip of paper. All it had on it was CX-ATEHWM. There was another line under it, but that one had been erased. Great. A code. I shoved the paper into my pocket and hoped I'd never need to look at it again.

Finally, I checked the fast food bag. I wasn't hungry, of course—except for information. There were three dinners in the bag. That was bad news. Unless Gregor Smetchinski had a monstrous appetite, this meant I had two more guys to deal with. And no idea how to do that.

There was a tunnel on the other side of the door. It led to another hallway. I crept down to the end of the tunnel and listened. I heard voices from one end, but they didn't seem very close. I got down on the floor and peeked past the end of the tunnel. About twenty feet to my left, I saw a closed door with a sliding bolt on it. I figured Mr. Murphy was locked inside. There was a door right across the hall from me with some sort of keypad lock. A small red light blinked below the numbers. There was another room at the other end of the hall. That door was open. I saw two guys in there, sitting at a table, talking. While I was watching, they got up and started walking down the hall.

I slipped deeper into the tunnel. The two men walked by me. They looked pretty big. I thought about trying to scare them, but I didn't see anything they might run into. I heard the bolt slide open. There was some shuffling and grunting.

A moment later, they came past me, dragging Mr. Murphy between them.

"Last chance to talk," one of them said.

I waited until they'd gone by, then peeked out. They were tying Mr. Murphy to a chair. They'd left the door open at the other end. I saw a bed in there with straps on it.

I slipped back down the tunnel, and through the door to the room with the tables. I needed to be where they couldn't hear me. I pulled out the iClotz and set it to record. I waited thirty seconds—that seemed long enough—and then started talking.

After I'd made my recording, I went back to the end of the tunnel. I peeked out to make sure the two guys were busy with Mr. Murphy. *You've got one shot,* I told myself. If I missed, it was all over.

18

Let It Slide

It **would be** just like playing shuffleboard in gym class. I was good at that. I pressed PLAY on the iClotz, then leaned out and slid it down the hall, aiming for the open door.

Score!

It slid right in, all the way to the back of the wall. A moment later, the recording reached past the silent part and started playing my voice.

"Hey! You guys! You're totally ugly. Stupid, too."

It worked. Both guys went running past the tunnel toward the room at the end of the hall. As soon as they passed me, I got out and followed them, being careful not to make a sound. They didn't look back.

"Bet you can't find me. Don't look under the bed."

They raced inside. I slammed the door, then slid the bolt shut before they knew what happened. They both hurled themselves at the door, screaming at me. But there was nothing they could do. I'd caught them. I went to the other end of the hall.

Mr. Murphy was tied to the chair. His face was puffy, like he'd been slapped around a bit. He looked really tired—the way my dad does when he's been working long hours for a couple weeks in a row.

"Are you okay?"

He nodded. "No permanent damage."

I reached for the ropes, then paused. "I passed my physical. Totally fooled the doctor with some simple tricks."

"Good for you."

"I did it without being carved up by anyone."

"Very good. Are you trying to make some sort of point? Because if you are, I'd much rather discuss it with you elsewhere."

"Yeah, I have a point to make. I'm a person. I might be dead, but I have feelings."

Mr. Murphy smirked. "Bad choice of words."

"Stop that. You know what I mean. You can't just make plans for me like surgery and stuff. I'm not a lab rat.

I know I joined BUM, and you're in charge. But you have to promise to respect my body."

"I promise," Mr. Murphy said.

I stared at him. His promise was probably worthless. But we could discuss that some other time. I was new at being a spy, and I still needed lots of training, but something had changed between us. I untied the ropes.

"Do you have my phone?"

Mr. Murphy pointed across the room. "It's on the table with my phone."

I went over and saw the one thing that could strike terror in my heart. "It's in pieces!" My phone had been taken apart. The chips were lying there like dead rectangular bugs with shiny legs.

"Just leave it."

"No. My mom will totally kill me. I just got the phone last Christmas. I also got a half-hour lecture about responsibility. No way I'm going home without it."

"Bring the pieces. We can put it back together at BUM."

"Great," I muttered as I dropped the pieces into an empty fast food bag I'd found in the trash. "My new ringtone will be an explosion."

"No, your ringtone will be a shrill little whine. Boo-hoo. Poor me. You can share your feelings with me later. Let's snatch their computer files and get out of here. The bad guys report to their headquarters every evening.

When they don't check in, RABID will know something has gone wrong."

I untied him. He stood, took a half step, then fell back into the chair. I held out my hand. "Come on. Lean on me."

"You'll snap."

"I'm stronger than I look."

"Apparently." He got up again. I helped him down the hall to the locked door near the tunnel. This one had a ten-button keypad on it, with the numbers from 0 to 9. The pad was right over the knob. I tried the knob. It wouldn't turn, so I rattled it.

"Have you ever seen a locked door spring open when you rattled the knob?" Mr. Murphy asked.

"Nope."

"Feel free to keep trying. Who knows? Maybe this one is different. Maybe it will magically rattle open."

I couldn't believe someone who had just been questioned for nearly twenty-four hours still had the strength to make fun of me. I let go of the knob. I'd show him. One way or another, I was going to find a way into that room. What would a spy do? I thought about some of the movies I'd seen.

"We could kick it down," I said.

"It's a reinforced metal door, Nathan. But go ahead and try if you're curious to see what happens when your zombie toes meet three inches of hardened steel."

"You'd enjoy that, wouldn't you?"

He shrugged. "Misery loves company. At the moment, I'm fairly miserable."

"You sure are," I muttered.

But he was right—kicking the door wouldn't do any good. I reached in my pocket and pulled out the keys. They wouldn't do any good. There was no keyhole in the door. But when I put the keys back, I felt something else.

"Hey, I found this in Smetchinski's pocket." I fished out the piece of paper and showed it to Mr. Murphy. "You're supposed to be good at codes. Figure it out."

"CXATEHWM." Mr. Murphy studied the paper for a moment. "It looks like there were numbers, but he erased them. Too bad we aren't at BUM. The lab could decipher it easily." He handed the slip back to me. "Here—your eyes are better than mine. Hold it at an angle. Sometimes, in indirect light, you can see the indentations left behind by the pencil."

I tilted the paper and squinted. He was right. I could make out the first three numbers. "Two, nine, then maybe another two . . ." I kept trying, but that was all I could see.

"Let's get out of here," Mr. Murphy said. "We need to call in the feds so they can take custody of these men."

"But we need that computer. And we still don't know what they're planning." I stared at the paper. There was something familiar about the letters and numbers.

"A good spy has to know when to get out," Mr. Murphy said. "It would be wonderful to have their files.

It would not be so wonderful to get captured again before we can call in some help."

"We know the first three numbers," I said. "CXA is two-nine-two."

"That's not enough to break the code," Mr. Murphy said. "Besides, C and A can't both stand for *two*, unless they're using a shifting encryption key or a one-time pad. There'd be no point doing that for a combination number. It has to be a simple code."

I wasn't listening too closely, because I'd finally figured out what was tickling around in my brain. "Got it!" I held the slip next to the pad while I typed some numbers—29283496.

"Nathan, stop playing around," Mr. Murphy said.

I heard a couple clicks, a whir, and the grinding sound of metal sliding against metal. The red light on the keypad turned green. The door popped open. Right after that, Mr. Murphy's jaw dropped open. It was a nice thing to see.

"How—?" He snatched the paper from my hand and stared at it. Then he stared at the keypad. "I don't understand."

"You probably don't send text messages," I said. "Most old people don't."

"I sent a text message once," Mr. Murphy said. "It's a very cumbersome process. And I'm not old."

"Right. Anyhow, the letters on the paper are the ones over the numbers on a phone. Any kid who texts a lot would figure it out. I don't need to see the letters. I know where they are. I can even text with my eyes closed." I pulled the door open the rest of the way.

There was a desk inside the room, with a laptop on it. I took the flash drive out of my pocket. But Mr. Murphy grabbed the laptop. "Let's go. We can do that in the car."

We headed back through the tunnel. Mr. Murphy leaned on me a bit, but I could tell he wanted to pretend he didn't need any help. He stopped when we got through the door, and looked at Smetchinski. "He'll be out for a while," Mr. Murphy said. "We'll have him and the other two picked up. With luck, RABID won't know we have the data from their computers for at least two or three hours. Maybe longer. This is a major success for us."

"What about the goop?" I asked. "Aren't they planning something big?" I thought about Smetchinski's words. *You're better off missing what's coming.*

"At this point, it's merely annoying. I think we can wait until tomorrow to clean things up." He raised the laptop. "The details are probably here. We'll inform the EPA, or whichever agency is best qualified to handle goop."

When I got near the car, Dr. Cushing shifted her eyes toward the trunk. I guess they'd all decided not to let Mr. Murphy know anything. That was a good idea. I just hoped Mookie could keep from blowing his cover.

"Are you all right, Peter?" Dr. Cushing asked.

"I'm fine." He slid into the backseat. I got in front.

133

"You don't look fine," Dr. Cushing said. "Let me check you out. I'm a doctor, remember?"

"It can wait. Nathan, give me the flash drive."

I passed it to him and he plugged it into the laptop. I guess he was sending the files to BUM.

Dr. Cushing called BUM to let them know we were out of the funeral parlor, then drove back toward East Craven. She and Mr. Murphy seemed to believe our mission was over. But I couldn't stop thinking about Smetchinski. It wasn't just the words or the way he said it. It was the look in his eyes. I could see pleasure in there. Pleasure from the pain and suffering of others.

I knew Mr. Murphy was exhausted, but I needed him to do something. "Can you just see what the plan was all about?" I asked. "I think it might be something bad."

"If it will keep you from whining." Mr. Murphy looked at some of the files on the laptop. "Here it is. The project is code-named Anubis. Whatever that is."

"I know!" I couldn't believe the one time I had a chance to show off, Abigail wasn't close enough to hear me. "That's the Egyptian god of the dead. Any fifth-grader could have told you that." I loved mythology. Egyptian, Greek, Norse, Aztec. It was all totally cool.

"Do you think RABID is planning something deadly?" Dr. Cushing asked.

"Unlikely," Mr. Murphy said. "They prefer to cause suffering. You can't rule dead people." He flashed me a grin. "With some exceptions, of course."

"Ha-ha. Very funny," I said. "You don't rule me."

"*Anubis* could refer to Smetchinski, since he runs funerals," Dr. Cushing said. "But it wouldn't hurt to make sure RABID's plan isn't more serious than we think. Nathan seems concerned, and I trust his instincts."

"Hmmmm," Mr. Murphy said. "I guess it's worth checking." He clicked through a couple more screens. About five minutes later, he said, "Take a look at this. It outlines their plan. Science is not my strong point."

He passed the laptop to Dr. Cushing, who'd pulled over to the side of the road. She read for a moment, then said, "Oh, dear. This is bad."

19

Growth Spurt

Bad?" **Mr. Murphy** leaned forward in his seat. "According to everything we've learned, the goop is a nuisance, but nothing more than that."

"I suspect the goop that's come through the water pipes so far is just a side effect of this creature they created." Dr. Cushing said.

"Creature?" Mr. Murphy asked.

"I'm not sure what to call it," Dr. Cushing said. "It's a life-form. One they created in a lab, specifically for this purpose. They spliced DNA from at least seven different sources into a central host."

She had his full attention now. "What's the danger?" Mr. Murphy asked.

"They've charted its growth with remote sensors. It's doubling in size every day. In a week, it will be one hundred twenty-eight times as big as it is now. If it isn't destroyed right away, it might become unstoppable."

"What will it do," he asked. "Clog up the pipes?"

"I fear it's a lot worse than that," Dr. Cushing said. "They've somehow combined a variety of fungi. Honey mushroom. Elfin saddle. Several others. Along with a slime mold. Strangely enough, there's also genetic material from bamboo and from willow trees. I haven't taken a botany class since college—but I know many types of fungi can make you sick."

I remembered what the plumber had told Mom. "Willows search out water," I said. "They even invade pipes."

"And bamboo is the fastest-growing plant," Dr. Cushing said. "This is looking very bad. I think it's designed to invade the water system and then make people sick. Does it say where the creature is located?"

Mr. Murphy tapped a few more keys. "There's an old sewage-treatment plant just north of East Craven, near the river. It was replaced by a new facility last year. I don't see any danger there. Sewer lines are separate from water pipes."

I knew the old plant. Everyone in town was complaining about how they hadn't removed the old sewage before they closed the plant. All the groups involved blamed each other, but nobody did anything about it. A large pond of sewage just sat there in the sun. Luckily, nobody lived too close to it. I didn't really care about any of that. I knew another thing about the plant that was a lot more important.

"That's right near the reservoir," I said.

"So there'd be major water pipes nearby for the creature to invade," Dr. Cushing said. "This is looking worse and worse."

"How do we destroy it?" Mr. Murphy asked.

"I'm not sure," Dr. Cushing said. "I'm not an expert on fungi. And I know even less about slime mold."

"One of my friends knows a lot about fungi," I said. I caught Dr. Cushing's eye, then glanced toward the trunk. "One of my closest friends. Very, very close. Probably one of my two closest friends at the moment."

"Nathan, we don't care about your social circle right now," Mr. Murphy said. "We're trying to prevent a disaster."

"Leave it to us, Nathan," Dr. Cushing said.

I was afraid she didn't understand. But then she said, "Your clothes are all ripped. You must be cold. I think I have a jacket in the trunk." Still holding the laptop, she hopped out of the car and went around to the back. I saw the trunk pop open. A moment later, Dr. Cushing closed the trunk and returned, carrying Mookie's jacket but no computer.

"Here. This should keep you warm." She handed me the jacket.

"Where's the laptop?" Mr. Murphy asked.

"Oh, dear—I guess I left it in the trunk," Dr. Cushing said. "But I saw enough to understand there's a problem. Now I need to think up a solution."

I realized she'd left the report with Abigail. I hoped Abigail was a fast reader. And a really fast thinker. Dr. Cushing started the car. "We better get back to East Craven. With luck, I'll have a plan by the time we reach the old sewage-treatment plant."

Sewage. Yay. I had a funny feeling I knew what my role would be in all of this. I could almost hear a thousand toilets flushing right over my head.

"Don't worry," Dr. Cushing said. I guess she knew what I was thinking. "That's where the creature is, but I don't think you'll actually have to go through any sewage."

She drove for a couple miles, then pulled over to the side of the road. "I guess I shouldn't leave the laptop back there."

"Scientists," Mr. Murphy muttered as Dr. Cushing walked behind the car. "They are such scatterbrains."

"Yeah. They aren't action people like us spies. I'll bet you've had some amazing adventures." I figured if I kept him talking, he wouldn't pay so much attention to what Dr. Cushing was doing. Instead of telling me about his adventures, he gave me a lecture about how spies need to keep secrets.

Dr. Cushing came back a minute or two later, carrying the laptop. I could tell she was also carrying a bunch of information she got from Abigail. "I'm almost positive now that there's an immediate danger. I remembered that elfin saddle is toxic. It causes vomiting and diarrhea. The honey mushroom spreads out underground, forming the largest life-form on the planet. This creature will spread through the water supply and make people sick."

"That just came to you?" Mr. Murphy asked.

"My memory isn't as sharp as a fifth-grader's." Dr. Cushing winked at me. "What really matters is I think I've figured out how to destroy the creature. A normal slime mold reacts to heat shock by retracting. But because of the genetic splicing from more solid life-forms, such as trees, the creature is denser than normal. If we can introduce a small concentrated heat source right in the center of the mass, we'll stress the entire organism and produce a chain reaction that will destroy it. If only we had a concentrated heat source."

"Are you sure?" Mr. Murphy asked.

"I'd better be. Once it grows much larger, it will be too late. We probably have less than an hour." She glanced over at me. Then she said it again. "If only we had a heat source."

She kept glancing at me, which made me nervous since she was driving. Then she poked me in the shoulder. "It would be great to have a heat source."

"Oh!" I guess Abigail had told Dr. Cushing about the

gumballs. I reached in my pocket. "Hey—I just remembered I have this." I explained to them about my doctor's appointment.

"We can call in some scuba divers to deliver it," Mr. Murphy said. "They could safely go inside this slime creature."

"By the time they got there, it could be too late," Dr. Cushing said. "And their body heat would trigger a defense reaction from the creature. The heat has to be activated at the very center of its mass, or it won't work. We have to count on Nathan. It won't react to him."

"I'm in," I said. "It doesn't sound bad." I was kind of excited about seeing a giant slime monster. Killer slime. Who wouldn't be excited?

"It will be unpleasant," Dr. Cushing said. "But it shouldn't be dangerous."

"Hey, I like a little danger." I relaxed in my seat, happy to know the hard part of this mission was over. I checked the backseat. Mr. Murphy was asleep. I guess the hard part of his mission was over, too. His part had definitely been a lot worse than mine.

A moment later, Mr. Murphy gasped. "What is that dreadful smell?"

Dr. Cushing and I glanced at each other. "I don't smell anything," I said.

"Neither do I," Dr. Cushing said.

I thought I heard a moan coming from the trunk.

Mr. Murphy sniffed again. "It's not just sewage. It smells like vomit, too."

"Rest up, Peter," Dr. Cushing said. "You've had a brutal day. You're probably suffering from sleep deprivation. That can cause you to imagine things. I'm going to drop you off at the East Craven access to BUM. It's on the way. You really need to get medical attention."

I thought Mr. Murphy was going to argue. But he nodded. I guess he was in pretty bad shape. He passed the laptop to me. "There might be more information about the sewer plant in one of the files. Have Dr. Cushing take a look before you go in."

"Thanks." I glanced toward the trunk again. Poor Abigail. I was going to have to get BUM to buy something real nice for her to make up for this. Maybe a microscope or something.

When we reached the museum, I handed Mr. Murphy the bag with the phone pieces.

"I'll have it reassembled," he said.

"No extra parts," I said. "No surprises. I don't want it blowing up in my pocket the next time it rings."

He took the bag and got out of the car. I expected him to thank me for rescuing him, but he just walked off.

Dr. Cushing drove around the corner, then stopped. We ran back to the trunk. Abigail looked almost as bad as Mr. Murphy had. She was pale. Her hair was straggly. And she'd lost her lunch all over her dress and the trunk. She glared at Mookie as they climbed out.

"Sorry," he said. "I tried to hold it. But it got to be too much. Maybe it would be better if I let out a little at a time."

"The word *better* doesn't belong in any discussion of your flatulence," Abigail said.

"Flatulence?" Mookie said. "It's not nice to make fun of my weight."

Abigail groaned, then turned toward me. "What happened so far?"

I filled her in as we drove north through East Craven to the old sewer plant. While I was talking, Abigail looked at files on the laptop.

"Ohmygosh," she said. "I found the plans for the place. The creature is in an enormous vat in the lowest level. But the whole plant is filled with deadly traps. I guess they didn't want anyone getting near the creature before it grew large enough to overflow the vat."

"How deadly?" I asked.

"Poison gas. Scalding steam. Thrusting pistons," she said.

"Cool," Mookie said. "It sounds like a video game."

"It sounds too dangerous," Abigail said. "You can't go in there."

"What happens if I don't?"

"A lot of people will get very sick," she said. "It will be like having a really bad stomach virus. The worst part is, one of the first symptoms will be extreme thirst. So people will drink even more of the contaminated water, and get even sicker."

"No problem," Mookie said. "We'll drink soda instead."

"Which is made of water," Abigail told him.

"So I have to go." I thought about the last time I'd had a stomach virus. It had been awful. And messy.

Abigail didn't argue. Neither did Dr. Cushing.

We pulled into the parking lot of the old sewer plant. There was tall grass growing around the fence, and the asphalt was cracked in a bunch of places. Dr. Cushing wrinkled her nose. There was an open pool of sewage far to one side.

"I think I found your brother," I told Mookie.

He sniffed. "Nope. Just a cousin."

The building was on the other side of the parking lot. I was glad I didn't have to wade through sewage or anything gunky.

"Do you have any sort of radio?" Abigail asked Dr. Cushing. "It would be good if we could stay in touch with Nathan."

"Just my phone," she said. "Do you have one?"

"It's back at my place," Abigail said. "Remember?"

"Mine's in pieces," I said.

"My folks won't get me one," Mookie said.

"I have an idea," Abigail said. "But you're not going to like it."

She explained what she had in mind. She was right. I didn't like it.

20

Slime Time

Maybe I could just take the laptop with me," I said.

"You can't carry it," Abigail said. "You'll need your hands for balance. And the environment inside the plant would stop it from working. Laptops don't like steam. This is the only way."

"The glue is for bones," I said.

"It will work on cartilage," she said. "Besides, it repairs the flesh around the broken bones. There's no reason it wouldn't work."

I knew she was right. No point stalling—especially

when there was a slime monster down there, growing larger by the minute.

I grabbed my left ear. "You realize Rodney would love to do this." He'd tried. Luckily, he'd failed.

I yanked on my ear. It ripped off way too easily. That bothered me. I put the ear on the dashboard in front of Dr. Cushing.

"I should be able hear you," I said. "Just like I can move my finger after it breaks off. Everything still acts like it's connected. I just wish you could hear me."

"Maybe we can," she said. "Our voices vibrate through our skulls. It's possible the sound will come through your ear. Try it."

I got out and stepped away from the car.

"Can you hear me?"

Dr. Cushing's voice came through the left side of my head, where my ear had been. I was hearing her through the ear in the car. "Yeah. Loud and clear. Can you hear me?"

I saw Dr. Cushing pick up my ear and hold it close to her own ear. I repeated the question.

"It's faint, but I hear you. I guess it's time to go in."

"Guess so."

"Good luck," she said.

The door was locked. But I still had Smetchinski's keys. I found one that worked.

I walked into the old plant. There was some sludge

on the floor, and a lot of flies. "I see three doors across from me," I said.

"Abigail says to take the middle one." Dr. Cushing's voice came through just fine.

I heard a buzzing close to my ear. There were flies on my shoulder. More landed on my arms. One crawled across the back of my hand. I guess, to them, I was just more dead meat. I hoped they weren't planning to lay eggs in me. I went to the middle door. There was a wheel on the outside, like on a ship's hatch, and a sign on the wall with a picture of a skull.

DANGER!
TOXIC ENVIRONMENT!
DO NOT ENTER!
☠

I told Dr. Cushing.

"You should be fine," she said.

I spun the wheel until the door opened, then went inside. The air was sort of green. I held up my hand to make sure the poison wasn't doing anything bad to my skin. The flies on my arm dropped like—well, like flies. I stood there for a moment, staring down at the floor. Someone who'd just walked in would have thought I'd spilled a large box of raisins.

There was one door in front of me, and one to the left. "Go left," Dr. Cushing said.

I went down a stairway and found myself in a room filled with large pipes. I started to walk through. "Here I go."

"Wait!" Dr. Cushing shouted.

A blast of steam shot out from the pipe right in front of me. I couldn't feel the heat, but I was pretty sure it was hot enough to fry my face. Though I guess *fry* wasn't the right word. I didn't even know what you called it when you steamed meat. Whatever you called it, I didn't want it happening to my face.

"There's hot steam," I told Dr. Cushing.

"There doesn't seem to be any way to shut it off," she said. "It looks like it's driven by a series of turbines. So there should be some sort of pattern. But it might be complicated. See if you can figure it out."

I watched the nearest pipe. After a short pause, another burst came out. Then there were two quick bursts. There was a definite pattern. I looked past it, to the next pipe. It was following the same pattern, but slightly later. So were all the pipes. I could get through, as long as I could time my moves just right.

I looked at my watch. The second hand sat there, as dead as a zombie. I guess the steamy air had killed it. That didn't matter. I'd practiced my fake pulse so much, I had a feel for the timing. I waited until I knew the biggest gap was about to come at the first pipe, then started to make my way across the room.

If there was ever a place where it was good not to be

nervous, this was it. The worst part was, I probably wouldn't even know I was getting burned until my face started to fall off like meat from an overcooked sparerib. So I had to be extra careful. But I got across without being blasted.

"Made it," I said. I took a sniff, just to be sure. It didn't smell like someone had just cooked dinner. That was a relief. I reached the next door. There was only one this time. Sludge, steam, poison gas . . . What next?

I opened the door and found out.

I faced some kind of huge engine with all sorts of moving parts. Gears and wheels were spinning. Shafts stuck out, whipping through the air like baseball bats. Pistons thrust out into the walkway. This was not a great place for a kid with weak bones. I didn't want to get hit out of the park. There was one path down the middle. But there was stuff whipping out across it from both sides. I guess RABID loved deadly traps as much as BUM loved exploding robots.

"Any advice?" I said.

"Watch your step," Dr. Cushing said. "I wish I had something better to suggest."

Watch your step. Those were the words that helped me figure out I could see in different directions with each eye. I moved up to the edge of the path and let my eyes drift to the sides.

Don't mess up.

I wanted to run through as fast as I could. But I knew,

from all the games I'd played, how that strategy only works once in a while, and is really only good if you just reached a checkpoint. You make a dash and hope you get lucky. If not, you try again. This wasn't a game. I didn't have infinite chances. I didn't even have a checkpoint. I had to do it right the first time.

I inched forward. A piston shot toward my head from the left. I ducked, waited, then stood and moved on. A chain whipped across the floor from the right. I jumped and let it pass under me.

The rest of the way across, I ducked, leaned, jumped, and twisted. If I hadn't been able to see both sides at once, I would never have made it. Finally, I reached another door.

"I'm still in one piece," I said. I almost expected a score to appear on the wall.

"Good. The creature should be down below."

End of the level. Time to face the boss. I opened the door, walked through it, and found myself on a small ledge high above the floor. There was a gigantic vat below me, almost two stories high. The creature was there, filling the whole vat and quivering. It was the color of weak iced tea. I saw thin threads of dark green running through it, branching out from the center like the veins in Smetchinski's eyes. Some of them went all the way to the surface. Green goop trickled from those spots. Dozens of blobs of goop, like tiny slugs, oozed over the rim of the vat, down the sides, and across the floor.

Mushroom poop.

At the center of the slime monster, something glowed and pulsed, like a heart made of jelly. That's where I had to go.

"This is it," I said.

"Be careful," Dr. Cushing said.

What was the careful way to get to the center of a gigantic modified slime mold? I didn't know. But I knew the quickest way. The top was only about five feet below me. I'd spent a lot of time at the town swimming pool last summer. I knew how to dive.

"Wait," Dr. Cushing said.

"What?"

"Abigail wanted me to warn you that the reaction to the heat might be a bit more violent than she originally thought."

"Great. I'll keep that in mind."

I could see the creature growing right in front of my eyes. It would spill out of the vat soon. I didn't have any time to think about what I was doing. I jumped up as high as I could and dived toward the vat of slime.

At that instant, I wasn't sure whether I was acting like a hero or an idiot.

21

☠

Down to Earth

It was like diving into pudding. My momentum took me halfway to the glowing spot. I kicked my feet. My body moved forward. The slime around me seemed to ripple. Some of the dark green tendrils wriggled toward me. A couple wrapped around my legs. I used my arms and swam hard for the center.

I reached into my pocket and grabbed one of the gumballs. *Here goes.* I gave it a squeeze. Instead of breaking, it shot out from between my thumb and first finger.

Great. Just great.

Luckily, it only went a few inches. I grabbed it and tried again, wrapping my other hand around my fingers so I could keep my grip on the gumball. I squeezed. It didn't break. I squeezed harder. It still didn't break.

The tendrils were pulling my legs in two directions, like a wishbone. More were coming. I needed to break the gumball right away. But my fingers weren't strong enough. There was nothing solid I could use to stomp it. I only had one choice.

I held the gumball up to my mouth and pushed it through my lips, trying to keep them as tightly sealed around it as possible. I didn't want slime mold pouring into my mouth.

My stomach didn't quiver, but my brain felt like it was gagging. I bit down on the gumball just enough to crack it, then spat it back into my hand.

I pushed it into the center of the goop, then crushed it, releasing the heat.

I heard a sound like Mookie's stomach makes when he's hungry. Except the rumble was a thousand times louder, and all around me. The slime at the center turned from light yellow to dark red. It was pulling together, growing thicker. All the slime rushed inward and swept past me. It was like I'd gotten caught in a rough ocean wave. The slime got darker, shifting from weak tea to tomato juice. Then it flashed and burst outward.

Abigail was right. It was a violent reaction.

I felt like I'd been thumped in the chest. By a truck. Everything shot upward. The goop burst toward the ceiling and punched through. It just blew apart the ceiling like it was made of straw. I was carried along with it.

High.

And then higher.

And then, unfortunately, even higher.

If I didn't have to worry about coming back down, I would have totally enjoyed the trip up. But coming down was definitely not going to be fun. I'd already passed the tops of the trees. I was riding on a wave of exploding goop. I guess I'd been shot up at an angle. I could see the broken roof of the building below me, to my left. To my right, a lot farther over, I could see the pool of sewage in the old treatment pond.

It looked like I was going to fall right between them, in the parking lot.

There was no way my bones would survive that. Or my skin. I'd burst like a plastic bag full of baked beans. I knew exactly what that looked like, since Mookie had brought a bag of beans for lunch once and managed to drop it on the cafeteria floor. I wondered whether my brain would keep on working after it was smeared across the parking lot.

I hoped, at least, I wouldn't land on Dr. Cushing's cool car.

If only there were some way I could glide over toward the sewage, I might have a chance. I'd seen pictures of skydivers gliding before they pulled their chutes, but I had no idea how they did it, and I had an incredibly short amount of time left to learn new skills.

I'd stopped rising and had started to fall. Wind whipped past my face. I tried tilting my body toward the sewage. Nothing happened except I began to tumble.

My torn pants legs flapped like kite tails. Mookie's jacket fluttered open on either side of me, like useless wings.

Useless?

Maybe not. I remembered Mookie running around, flapping his jacket. MookieHawk. I wondered whether the jacket would be enough to let me control my direction a little. That's all I needed—just a nudge toward the sewage pool.

I grabbed the bottom edges of the jacket in each hand and stretched my arms out, like Mookie did on the playground—and like I used to do when I was little and I wanted to play superhero. Wings. I had wings. Sort of. They seemed to catch some air. Not enough to slow me much, but enough that I could sort of glide.

I slid through the air, more like an uncoordinated flying squirrel than a bird, trying to angle toward the sewage pool. I spotted the car. Dr. Cushing was standing outside the driver's door, staring up. Even from far above, I could tell her face was pale from fright. Abigail and Mookie got out to join her. Abigail was pale, too. With Mookie standing between them, they looked like a tomato sandwich.

"Slow down!" Mookie screamed.

"I'd love to!" I was plunging faster and faster. I remembered something from science. The longer you fall, the faster you go. Abigail would be able to figure out exactly how fast I was falling. I didn't have time for that.

I swooped over some more and tried to figure out how long to keep swooping. I didn't want to go too far and fly right past the sewage pond. There was a big metal walkway on the other side. That would mess me up just as badly as the parking lot.

The wind ripped the jacket from my grip. It got yanked right off my body. But I was over the sewage. I tried to rotate so I went in feetfirst. This wasn't the place for a dive.

It sort of worked. I splashed into the wet muck at an angle, but I was straight enough so I didn't do a belly flop. The sewage felt almost as thick as the slime monster. I closed my eyes and clamped my lips shut. I felt lumps bouncing off my feet and legs as I plunged deeper. I didn't even want to think about what they were made of. Something else smacked me in the face. The lower I got, the thicker the sludge seemed to be. My plunge stopped just as my feet hit the bottom.

"I made it!" I gasped.

Nooooo!!!!! Bad move. I slammed my mouth shut and swam for the surface. Then I paddled over to the edge of the pool and spat out as much as I could.

Dr. Cushing met me by the fence. "Are you okay?" she asked as I started to climb over to her side.

"I think so." I looked down at my body for any sign of broken bones. It was hard to tell. I was pretty much painted with sewage from head to toe, over a coating of mutated slime monster.

"That was amazing," Abigail said.

"Next time, I want to go with you," Mookie said. "That looked awesome. You were flying!"

"It's not as much fun as it looks," I said. I glanced back at the sewage pond, then pointed to where Mookie's jacket was floating on top. "You want me to get it?"

"Nah. That's okay. My mom just won another one, and it's even cooler."

"Hard to imagine," I said.

"I was so worried about you." Dr. Cushing reached out like she was going to give me a hug, but then paused and backed off a step.

I couldn't blame her. "Maybe I'll just take a quick dip in the river."

"Good idea," she said.

I crossed the street and went down the bank. I didn't like the idea of washing sewage into the water, but I figured I'd just saved the whole East Coast, or maybe even the whole country, from losing all their fresh water. I washed off, rinsed my mouth a half-dozen times, then went back to the car.

Dr. Cushing handed me my ear. I got out my glue, spread some on the torn edges of the ear, then stuck it back where it belonged.

I screamed, like I always do. It hurts a lot.

"Oh, dear," Dr. Cushing said. "Is it always that painful?"

"Yeah. It's bad. At least it doesn't last long."

She looked over at Abigail. "I think I know what our first project should be."

"Absolutely," Abigail said. "I've already started considering approaches. We don't want to inhibit the regeneration, but we need to inhibit the neurotransmitters."

"Or block the receptors," Dr. Cushing said.

Their eyes lit up. They kept talking. I didn't listen, since I knew I wouldn't understand any of it. But I was happy to see them so excited.

"Tell me about the monster," Mookie said.

So while the two scientists discussed neurons and stuff, Mookie and I talked about the things that excited us.

Dr. Cushing dropped off Abigail and Mookie on the way to the museum. I had a feeling the first thing Abigail would do was take a shower. Or maybe rinse out her nose with a garden hose. The first thing Mookie would do would be to get a snack. The fact that he'd been hanging out near large amounts of sewage wouldn't hurt his appetite.

Dr. Cushing parked the car in front of the museum. "You can give us a report before you go home, Nathan."

I looked at the shredded remains of my pants and shirt. "What about clothes?"

"We've already gathered some from your room," she said. "What good is a whole espionage organization if we can't manage to provide clean clothes for one of our own?"

"Thanks." *One of our own.* I liked the sound of that.

"We can get you a duplicate jacket, but that will have to wait until tomorrow."

"No problem," I said. "Mom's used to me forgetting my jacket."

We went into the Museum of Tile and Grout. Mr. Murphy was sitting there, in a chair next to the desk, waiting for us.

"Peter, I thought you were going to get medical attention."

"I wanted to wait for Nathan. We never leave someone in the field." He looked at me, then sniffed. "This time, I definitely smell sewage."

"That would be me," I said.

He pointed toward the elevator and told Dr. Cushing, "After you."

She got in. "I'll see you superspies on the other side."

The door closed. The car shot off. I knew it would be a couple minutes before it came back.

I looked at Mr. Murphy. His eyes were half-closed. He seemed to be totally exhausted, and not interested in talking. That was okay. I didn't mind silence.

But a moment later, he said, "Nathan?"

"Yeah?"

"You'll be a good spy. A very good spy."

"Thanks."

"Once I've trained you a bit more, of course."

"Of course."

"Make that a lot more."

"Whatever you say."

"Now you're mocking me."

"I wouldn't dream of it."

"You seem to dream of nothing else. And, by the way, I'm not old."

"I never said you were."

"You implied it."

"I don't even know what that means."

"That's because you're young and inexperienced."

"It's good to be young."

"Do you really want to hear stories about my adventures?"

"I'd love to."

The elevator door opened. He let me go first. I didn't argue. Not too much, at least.

Later

So I'd had my first chance to be a spy. I'd gotten through my doctor's appointment. And I'd saved millions of people from spending a lot of time in the bathroom. Not a bad week.

The computer files I'd stolen had tons of useful information about RABID. BUM was able to give a lot of help to our government, and to several other countries. They also fixed my phone. I don't think they added anything to it, since it hasn't exploded so far, but I'm not completely sure about that. They also got Mookie's iClotz back.

All the water is fine now. The goop is gone. Even so,

Ferdinand didn't take a shower for two whole weeks. That was definitely not a good thing.

Mr. Murphy hasn't changed. He still bosses me around and makes fun of me when I mess up. He's always smirking and giggling. He never really thanked me for saving him. But every once in a while, when he doesn't think I'm watching, I catch him looking at me with a little bit of a friendly smile.

I haven't told him what I can do with my eyes. After all, spies work on a need-to-know basis. Especially superspies.

Mookie is still grinning from being called brilliant by both Abigail and Dr. Cushing. He's never going to let me forget about that. His new jacket has orange and white stripes. It's a little too small for him, so he looks like a piece of saltwater taffy. But he loves the logo on the back for Yaggie's Candy-Coated Sardine Chips.

Abigail and Dr. Cushing have become e-mail pals. Neither of them seems to be worried about the security of e-mail. I have a feeling I wouldn't understand most of the things they talk about. I know they're working on the problem of painless bone glue, and also a bone-strengthening machine that won't blow me into a billion pieces. If anyone can make that stuff work, they can. Dr. Cushing gave Abigail a gas chromatograph. Whatever that is.

Rodney and Mr. Lomux are back. That's not good. I think they both sort of blame me for what happened to them, even though they have no idea what really went on that day. Somehow, Abigail's last heat-up gumball got slipped into Rodney's back pocket when he was about to sit down in the cafeteria on Friday. I have no idea who might have done that. Someone sneaky, I guess. Maybe someone with cool spy skills and very steady hands.

Dad and I played pool that weekend. We had a great time. It turns out I'm pretty good. As I said, I do have a steady hand. And a dead eye.

There are lots of other dangerous groups out there for BUM to fight. And RABID is far from out of the picture. They probably hate BUM now even more than ever. I'm sure they're going to keep me busy. But I'm glad about that. It's nice being useful.

I guess Dad's right. Life is good. Giga-good. No, make that tera-good.

TURN THE PAGE
FOR A SNEAK PEEK AT

THE
BIG
STINK

Nathan Abercrombie,
Accidental Zombie

BOOK FOUR

1

Raising a Stink

"This stinks," Mookie said.

"It certainly rots," Abigail said.

I had to agree—it wasn't a good situation. But, compared to being turned into a walking dead kid, it wasn't a big deal, so I tried to look on the bright side. "At least it's only for a week or two." I shifted around in the tiny seat. If I crossed my feet, I could barely fit my legs under the little desk. I almost felt like I was wearing it.

"Hey, you know what? We can pretend we're giants." Mookie grabbed his desk with one hand and lifted it up a couple inches. Then he growled and shook it.

"Cool. I hadn't thought of that." I stared at my desk

and pretended it was normal sized and I was huge. That was fun. Down at the boardwalk in Wildwood, they have this giant chair. You can sit in it and get your picture taken. They have a giant pencil you can hold, too. It makes you look like a miniature person. I guess this was the opposite. The miniature desk and chair made me look like a giant.

"Well, fee fie yippee foe fum," Abigail said. "That makes it all better."

"I smell the blood of an Englishman." Mookie sniffed. "No, wait. My mistake. I smell last night's bean soup."

"Ew." Abigail slipped out of her seat, staggered away from Mookie, and sat at the empty desk on the other side of me. "Mookie, you need to register your digestive system with the government as a toxic waste dump."

He patted his gut. "It's more like a national monument." He sniffed again. "Actually, I can't smell anything. I think I'm getting a cold. But you don't see me acting all grumpy."

"Yeah, what's up?" I asked Abigail. "You don't normally complain this much."

"This place brings back too many bad memories," she said. "I never thought I'd have to revisit them."

"It's all good memories for me," Mookie said. "Crayons, songs, puppets. Tons of good stuff. Especially the cupcakes. I remember lots of cupcakes." He smacked my shoulder. "Remember?"

I thought back. "Sure. With big globs of icing."

"Parents baked them every time someone had a birthday." Mookie said. "I had three birthdays one year because Mom won two hundred cupcakes in a radio contest and she wanted to get rid of them. I guess nobody kept track. Or they just loved cupcakes as much as I do. We don't have cupcakes nearly enough, now. I miss this place."

I remembered those cupcakes. They were green. I think they were made with broccoli or zucchini or something. But almost anything tastes great if it has enough icing on it, so nobody complained.

Mookie stood up on his chair and shouted, "Hey, any birthdays coming up? Don't forget the cupcakes. You have to bring them. It's a rule here."

I guess I had good and bad memories, which kind of canceled each other out. Back then, the art teacher was always putting my stuff on the display board and telling me I had talent. I'd had a mean first-grade teacher who yelled at all the kids and smelled like mouthwash, but she quit, and the teacher who took over for her was really nice. So, unlike Abigail, I didn't mind being here again—except that everything was too small for us fifth graders. Not only were the chairs and desks tiny, but the water fountains were so low they looked like they were made for dogs.

"Hey, come on. Birthdays?" Mookie shouted. He

stepped up on the desk. I heard it groan, but it didn't break. "It doesn't have to be right now. It can be any time this month."

The bell rang and Ms. Otranto, our language, arts, and social studies teacher, walked into the room. She stared at Mookie.

"Sorry," he said as he climbed off his desk and sat back down. "I was taking a poll."

As Ms. Otranto walked toward the desk in front, which was full sized, she looked up at the drawings of nursery-rhyme characters that lined the wall above the blackboard, sighed, and said pretty much the same thing I'd just said. "Don't worry, class. It's just for one or two weeks. We should be happy they had room for us. All the other fifth graders have to double up and share class-rooms."

So there we were, crammed into a first-grade class-room at Borloff Lower Elementary School while our own school—Belgosi Upper Elementary—got cleaned and disinfected. Apparently, the building had developed some sort of dangerous mold spore problem, thanks to the leak in the cafeteria ceiling. This had nothing to do with the giant slime mold I'd run into—actually, dived into—the other week. It was something that had happened to a lot of schools in the state. Either way, we were stuck here until the Board of Health said it was safe to go back to Belgosi.

Mold spores aren't good for kids to breathe. That's

not a problem for me. I don't need to breathe. I could sit at the bottom of the ocean for a month without any problem. I could walk through a cloud of poison gas and not even blink. Mookie could turn every pot of bean soup in the whole universe into toxic gas bombs and I wouldn't care.

I'm sort of half dead. I've been like that since my friend Abigail's mad-scientist uncle accidentally splashed me with a whole bunch of Hurt-Be-Gone. I don't feel pain. I don't need to sleep. I don't have a heartbeat, either.

As for being giants, I have to say Mookie nailed it with that description. Not only were the chairs and everything really small, but so were the Borloff kids. At Belgosi, we were already the big kids. Our school was for grades three through five. Being the fifth graders, we were the biggest kids in the place.

Here at Borloff, we got to walk through the halls to our classroom with kids from kindergarten, first, and second grade. The kindergartners seemed especially small. I was almost afraid that I'd step on one, or that Mookie would trip over his laces, stumble into a group of them in the hallway, and crush them like bugs. Mookie trips a lot.

So we were the giants. Until the real giants shuffled into our classroom. Twenty of them. Big and scary. They didn't look happy.

WRITING AND RESEARCH ACTIVITIES

I. Being Undead

A. Throughout the novel, Nathan reflects on his absent heartbeat, lost sense of pain, and other physical changes that come with being a zombie. Make a list of at least ten of these changes. Beside each item on the list, note the positive and/or negative aspects of this physical characteristic.

B. On page 113, Dr. Cushing refers to Nathan's lack of an "autonomic nervous system." After researching at the library or online, prepare an informational poster on the autonomic nervous system, including the sympathetic and parasympathetic systems, and the fight-or-flight reaction. Use this information as the basis for a group discussion as to whether the absence of an autonomic nervous system makes Nathan a better or worse spy than Peter Murphy.

C. Create an illustrated Zombie Handbook for kids who have accidentally become undead. Include a list of advantages and disadvantages of zombie life, tips for tricking people into thinking you're alive, situations to avoid, suggested ways to spend your unlimited waking hours, and repair ideas for zombie accidents.

D. One way to look at the Nathan Abercrombie series is as the result of the author asking a cool "what if" question: What if an unfortunate accident turned an ordinary kid into a half-dead zombie? Frame your own question by modifying the one above (perhaps substituting "werewolf," "genius," or "criminal mastermind" for "half-dead zombie"), or create an entirely new "what if." Write a short story, story summary, or novel chapter outline describing what would happen in your new "what if" situation. Give your story a catchy title.

II. Friends, Family, and Fungus

A. Becoming a zombie has made Nathan appreciate the friendship and support of Abigail and Mookie. In the character of Nathan, write a note to one of these friends thanking them for their help with the zombie situation. Or, write a short essay describing the way in which a friend was there for you during a difficult time.

B. In the character of Nathan, write a two-paragraph journal entry that begins, "It definitely isn't easy being dead around Mom (or Dad)."

C. Go online to find a recipe for "goop" and make a batch, adjusting food coloring and other specifics to try to match the descriptions of the substance in *Goop Soup* (links: http://multiples.about.com/cs/familyfun/ht/Goop.htm or http://www.makingfriends.com/r_goop.htm). Find a definition for a non-Newtonian fluid. Is goop such a fluid? Why or why not? Make a list of fun things to do with goop but be aware, it stains!

D. You are the RABID scientist who invented the toxic fungus threatening East Craven. Write a speech explaining how and why you accomplished this gross feat. Dressed as a mad scientist, present your speech to friends or classmates. Or, make a live-action or animated movie (complete with a set and special effects, such as goop, if desired) of your speech to share.

E. Write a poem or song entitled "Diving into Goop." Use details from Nathan's heroic fungus-jump and/or your own imagination to describe the sounds, smells, sights, tastes, and sensations of your dive, and your thoughts or feelings afterward.

III. Wordplay

A. Invite friends or classmates to submit their choices for the funniest line in the novel. Take a class vote to select the top three lines. Prepare a poster announcing the vote results, including the winning lines accompanied by funny illustrations.

B. The author uses many literary devices to create humor in his story. Make a list of *Goop Soup* chapter titles. Try to figure out what type of wordplay (such as hyperbole, irony, or juxtaposition) is at work in each one. Note that some of the jokes make sense in relation to what happens in the chapter. For example, "Stare Case" (chapter 4) is a pun beginning a chapter in which Nathan experiments with staring. Library or online resources may be useful.

C. Find a definition for the term "acronym." What words are used to form the acronyms BUM and RABID? On page 21, Mr. Murphy refers to some other evil organizations: SPLOTCH, GACK, MUCOUS, and PHLEGM. Create logical word sequences that would form these acronyms. Share your creations with friends or classmates.

D. How are the mathematical terms "mega," "giga," and "tera" put to clever use in the story? Go to the library or online to find the Latin and Greek origins of these words and other prefixes that denote units of measure, and some root words to which these prefixes are often attached (such as byte). On your own or in small groups, brainstorm a list of new words or phrases employing these prefixes (plus zocto, pico, zetta, yotta, and others) in fun, funny, or useful ways.

QUESTIONS FOR DISCUSSION

1. In the introduction to the novel, Nathan notes that "Life is simple. Death is tricky." In chapter 2, Nathan's dad tells him that "life is good." How are these observations both truthful and ironic in the context of the story? In what ways do you find life simple and/or good?

2. Compare Nathan's relationships with Peter Murphy and Dr. Cushing to his relationships with his parents. In what different ways do his parents and his BUM supervisors worry about Nathan? What secrets or concerns does Nathan keep from each of these people? Can you be totally honest with your parents or with other adults?

3. For what spy-related skills does Mr. Murphy test Nathan? How does Nathan handle these tests? How does he react to Abigail's observation that he isn't "used to failing anymore" (chapter 5)?

4. What are some of the unusual methods and technologies BUM uses to contact Nathan? What more common (and reliable) technologies does Mr. Murphy avoid and why? Which BUM device would you most like to use to communicate with your friends? What type of information would you share through this method?

5. What do Abigail's wall posters of Einstein and Monet tell you about her character? What does Mookie's love of his iClotz and favorite jacket tell you about him? What two items from the novel would you select to create a sense of Nathan's character? If you had to pick two objects or images to describe yourself to others, what would they be?

6. In what different ways do Mr. Murphy, Abigail, and Mookie each try to help Nathan develop a plan to trick his pediatrician, Dr. Scrivella, into thinking he is alive? How do their different strategies show readers what these characters consider to be the most important or difficult part of Nathan's zombie state? What else do their problem-solving techniques reveal?

7. The second part of the story focuses on Nathan's efforts to rescue Mr. Murphy by catching RABID agent and funeral director Smetchinski. Is there a relationship between these two problems? How does Nathan apply some of Abigail's inventions to both problems?

8. When does goop first appear in the novel? How do Nathan and his associates connect the goop problem to the trouble with RABID? What is RABID's evil plan for East Craven? Why is Nathan the only one who can carry out BUM's defense strategy? How have his failed spy tests given Nathan insights that help him succeed in this effort?

9. How does Nathan's relationship with Mr. Murphy change in the course of the story? Do you think the newfound friendship between Dr. Cushing and Abigail is a good thing? Explain your answers.

10. In a 2004 wordpress.com interview, David Lubar commented, "One of my favorite quotes . . . is from C. S. Lewis. He said, 'A book worth reading only in childhood is not worth reading even then'" (http:// entertheoctopus.wordpress.com/2009/09/04/interview-with-david-lubar-author-nathan-abercrombie-accidental-zombie-my-rotten-life/). Do you agree? To what adult would you most like to recommend this book and why?

11. On the final page of the novel, Nathan decides that life is "tera-good." What does this expression mean to Nathan? Is this observation made with the same sense of irony used in the quotes noted in question number 1? In what ways has Nathan's view of himself, "life," and being a zombie changed in the course of the story?